# JUST NOW

(A Cami Lark Mystery —Book Seven)

BLAKE PIERCE

**Blake Pierce**

Blake Pierce is the USA Today bestselling author of the RILEY PAGE mystery series, which includes seventeen books. Blake Pierce is also the author of the MACKENZIE WHITE mystery series, comprising fourteen books; of the AVERY BLACK mystery series, comprising six books; of the KERI LOCKE mystery series, comprising five books; of the MAKING OF RILEY PAIGE mystery series, comprising six books; of the KATE WISE mystery series, comprising seven books; of the CHLOE FINE psychological suspense mystery, comprising six books; of the JESSIE HUNT psychological suspense thriller series, comprising twenty-eight books; of the AU PAIR psychological suspense thriller series, comprising three books; of the ZOE PRIME mystery series, comprising six books; of the ADELE SHARP mystery series, comprising sixteen books, of the EUROPEAN VOYAGE cozy mystery series, comprising six books; of the LAURA FROST FBI suspense thriller, comprising eleven books; of the ELLA DARK FBI suspense thriller, comprising sixteen books (and counting); of the A YEAR IN EUROPE cozy mystery series, comprising nine books, of the AVA GOLD mystery series, comprising six books; of the RACHEL GIFT mystery series, comprising ten books (and counting); of the VALERIE LAW mystery series, comprising nine books (and counting); of the PAIGE KING mystery series, comprising eight books (and counting); of the MAY MOORE mystery series, comprising eleven books; of the CORA SHIELDS mystery series, comprising eight books (and counting); of the NICKY LYONS mystery series, comprising eight books (and counting), of the CAMI LARK mystery series, comprising eight books (and counting), of the AMBER YOUNG mystery series, comprising five books (and counting), of the DAISY FORTUNE mystery series, comprising five books (and counting), of the FIONA RED mystery series, comprising eight books (and counting), of the FAITH BOLD mystery series, comprising eight books (and counting), of the JULIETTE HART mystery series, comprising five books (and counting), of the MORGAN CROSS mystery series, comprising five books (and counting), and of the new FINN WRIGHT mystery series, comprising five books (and counting).

An avid reader and lifelong fan of the mystery and thriller genres, Blake loves to hear from you, so please feel free to visit www.blakepierceauthor.com to learn more and stay in touch.

ISBN: 978-1-0943-8236-4

**BOOKS BY BLAKE PIERCE**

**FINN WRIGHT MYSTERY SERIES**
WHEN YOU'RE MINE (Book #1)
WHEN YOU'RE SAFE (Book #2)
WHEN YOU'RE CLOSE (Book #3)
WHEN YOU'RE SLEEPING (Book #4)
WHEN YOU'RE SANE (Book #5)

**MORGAN CROSS MYSTERY SERIES**
FOR YOU (Book #1)
FOR RAGE (Book #2)
FOR LUST (Book #3)
FOR WRATH (Book #4)
FOREVER (Book #5)

**JULIETTE HART MYSTERY SERIES**
NOTHING TO FEAR (Book #1)
NOTHING THERE (Book #2)
NOTHING WATCHING (Book #3)
NOTHING HIDING (Book #4)
NOTHING LEFT (Book #5)

**FAITH BOLD MYSTERY SERIES**
SO LONG (Book #1)
SO COLD (Book #2)
SO SCARED (Book #3)
SO NORMAL (Book #4)
SO FAR GONE (Book #5)
SO LOST (Book #6)
SO ALONE (Book #7)
SO FORGOTTEN (Book #8)

**FIONA RED MYSTERY SERIES**
LET HER GO (Book #1)
LET HER BE (Book #2)
LET HER HOPE (Book #3)
LET HER WISH (Book #4)

LET HER LIVE (Book #5)
LET HER RUN (Book #6)
LET HER HIDE (Book #7)
LET HER BELIEVE (Book #8)

**DAISY FORTUNE MYSTERY SERIES**
NEED YOU (Book #1)
CLAIM YOU (Book #2)
CRAVE YOU (Book #3)
CHOOSE YOU (Book #4)
CHASE YOU (Book #5)

**AMBER YOUNG MYSTERY SERIES**
ABSENT PITY (Book #1)
ABSENT REMORSE (Book #2)
ABSENT FEELING (Book #3)
ABSENT MERCY (Book #4)
ABSENT REASON (Book #5)

**CAMI LARK MYSTERY SERIES**
JUST ME (Book #1)
JUST OUTSIDE (Book #2)
JUST RIGHT (Book #3)
JUST FORGET (Book #4)
JUST ONCE (Book #5)
JUST HIDE (Book #6)
JUST NOW (Book #7)
JUST HOPE (Book #8)

**NICKY LYONS MYSTERY SERIES**
ALL MINE (Book #1)
ALL HIS (Book #2)
ALL HE SEES (Book #3)
ALL ALONE (Book #4)
ALL FOR ONE (Book #5)
ALL HE TAKES (Book #6)
ALL FOR ME (Book #7)
ALL IN (Book #8)

**CORA SHIELDS MYSTERY SERIES**
UNDONE (Book #1)

UNWANTED (Book #2)
UNHINGED (Book #3)
UNSAID (Book #4)
UNGLUED (Book #5)
UNSTABLE (Book #6)
UNKNOWN (Book #7)
UNAWARE (Book #8)

**MAY MOORE SUSPENSE THRILLER**

NEVER RUN (Book #1)
NEVER TELL (Book #2)
NEVER LIVE (Book #3)
NEVER HIDE (Book #4)
NEVER FORGIVE (Book #5)
NEVER AGAIN (Book #6)
NEVER LOOK BACK (Book #7)
NEVER FORGET (Book #8)
NEVER LET GO (Book #9)
NEVER PRETEND (Book #10)
NEVER HESITATE (Book #11)

**PAIGE KING MYSTERY SERIES**

THE GIRL HE PINED (Book #1)
THE GIRL HE CHOSE (Book #2)
THE GIRL HE TOOK (Book #3)
THE GIRL HE WISHED (Book #4)
THE GIRL HE CROWNED (Book #5)
THE GIRL HE WATCHED (Book #6)
THE GIRL HE WANTED (Book #7)
THE GIRL HE CLAIMED (Book #8)

**VALERIE LAW MYSTERY SERIES**

NO MERCY (Book #1)
NO PITY (Book #2)
NO FEAR (Book #3)
NO SLEEP (Book #4)
NO QUARTER (Book #5)
NO CHANCE (Book #6)
NO REFUGE (Book #7)
NO GRACE (Book #8)
NO ESCAPE (Book #9)

**RACHEL GIFT MYSTERY SERIES**
HER LAST WISH (Book #1)
HER LAST CHANCE (Book #2)
HER LAST HOPE (Book #3)
HER LAST FEAR (Book #4)
HER LAST CHOICE (Book #5)
HER LAST BREATH (Book #6)
HER LAST MISTAKE (Book #7)
HER LAST DESIRE (Book #8)
HER LAST REGRET (Book #9)
HER LAST HOUR (Book #10)

**AVA GOLD MYSTERY SERIES**
CITY OF PREY (Book #1)
CITY OF FEAR (Book #2)
CITY OF BONES (Book #3)
CITY OF GHOSTS (Book #4)
CITY OF DEATH (Book #5)
CITY OF VICE (Book #6)

**A YEAR IN EUROPE**
A MURDER IN PARIS (Book #1)
DEATH IN FLORENCE (Book #2)
VENGEANCE IN VIENNA (Book #3)
A FATALITY IN SPAIN (Book #4)

**ELLA DARK FBI SUSPENSE THRILLER**
GIRL, ALONE (Book #1)
GIRL, TAKEN (Book #2)
GIRL, HUNTED (Book #3)
GIRL, SILENCED (Book #4)
GIRL, VANISHED (Book 5)
GIRL ERASED (Book #6)
GIRL, FORSAKEN (Book #7)
GIRL, TRAPPED (Book #8)
GIRL, EXPENDABLE (Book #9)
GIRL, ESCAPED (Book #10)
GIRL, HIS (Book #11)
GIRL, LURED (Book #12)
GIRL, MISSING (Book #13)

GIRL, UNKNOWN (Book #14)
GIRL, DECEIVED (Book #15)
GIRL, FORLORN (Book #16)

**LAURA FROST FBI SUSPENSE THRILLER**
ALREADY GONE (Book #1)
ALREADY SEEN (Book #2)
ALREADY TRAPPED (Book #3)
ALREADY MISSING (Book #4)
ALREADY DEAD (Book #5)
ALREADY TAKEN (Book #6)
ALREADY CHOSEN (Book #7)
ALREADY LOST (Book #8)
ALREADY HIS (Book #9)
ALREADY LURED (Book #10)
ALREADY COLD (Book #11)

**EUROPEAN VOYAGE COZY MYSTERY SERIES**
MURDER (AND BAKLAVA) (Book #1)
DEATH (AND APPLE STRUDEL) (Book #2)
CRIME (AND LAGER) (Book #3)
MISFORTUNE (AND GOUDA) (Book #4)
CALAMITY (AND A DANISH) (Book #5)
MAYHEM (AND HERRING) (Book #6)

**ADELE SHARP MYSTERY SERIES**
LEFT TO DIE (Book #1)
LEFT TO RUN (Book #2)
LEFT TO HIDE (Book #3)
LEFT TO KILL (Book #4)
LEFT TO MURDER (Book #5)
LEFT TO ENVY (Book #6)
LEFT TO LAPSE (Book #7)
LEFT TO VANISH (Book #8)
LEFT TO HUNT (Book #9)
LEFT TO FEAR (Book #10)
LEFT TO PREY (Book #11)
LEFT TO LURE (Book #12)
LEFT TO CRAVE (Book #13)
LEFT TO LOATHE (Book #14)
LEFT TO HARM (Book #15)

LEFT TO RUIN (Book #16)

**THE AU PAIR SERIES**

ALMOST GONE (Book#1)
ALMOST LOST (Book #2)
ALMOST DEAD (Book #3)

**ZOE PRIME MYSTERY SERIES**

FACE OF DEATH (Book#1)
FACE OF MURDER (Book #2)
FACE OF FEAR (Book #3)
FACE OF MADNESS (Book #4)
FACE OF FURY (Book #5)
FACE OF DARKNESS (Book #6)

**A JESSIE HUNT PSYCHOLOGICAL SUSPENSE SERIES**

THE PERFECT WIFE (Book #1)
THE PERFECT BLOCK (Book #2)
THE PERFECT HOUSE (Book #3)
THE PERFECT SMILE (Book #4)
THE PERFECT LIE (Book #5)
THE PERFECT LOOK (Book #6)
THE PERFECT AFFAIR (Book #7)
THE PERFECT ALIBI (Book #8)
THE PERFECT NEIGHBOR (Book #9)
THE PERFECT DISGUISE (Book #10)
THE PERFECT SECRET (Book #11)
THE PERFECT FAÇADE (Book #12)
THE PERFECT IMPRESSION (Book #13)
THE PERFECT DECEIT (Book #14)
THE PERFECT MISTRESS (Book #15)
THE PERFECT IMAGE (Book #16)
THE PERFECT VEIL (Book #17)
THE PERFECT INDISCRETION (Book #18)
THE PERFECT RUMOR (Book #19)
THE PERFECT COUPLE (Book #20)
THE PERFECT MURDER (Book #21)
THE PERFECT HUSBAND (Book #22)
THE PERFECT SCANDAL (Book #23)
THE PERFECT MASK (Book #24)
THE PERFECT RUSE (Book #25)

THE PERFECT VENEER (Book #26)
THE PERFECT PEOPLE (Book #27)
THE PERFECT WITNESS (Book #28)

**CHLOE FINE PSYCHOLOGICAL SUSPENSE SERIES**
NEXT DOOR (Book #1)
A NEIGHBOR'S LIE (Book #2)
CUL DE SAC (Book #3)
SILENT NEIGHBOR (Book #4)
HOMECOMING (Book #5)
TINTED WINDOWS (Book #6)

**KATE WISE MYSTERY SERIES**
IF SHE KNEW (Book #1)
IF SHE SAW (Book #2)
IF SHE RAN (Book #3)
IF SHE HID (Book #4)
IF SHE FLED (Book #5)
IF SHE FEARED (Book #6)
IF SHE HEARD (Book #7)

**THE MAKING OF RILEY PAIGE SERIES**
WATCHING (Book #1)
WAITING (Book #2)
LURING (Book #3)
TAKING (Book #4)
STALKING (Book #5)
KILLING (Book #6)

**RILEY PAIGE MYSTERY SERIES**
ONCE GONE (Book #1)
ONCE TAKEN (Book #2)
ONCE CRAVED (Book #3)
ONCE LURED (Book #4)
ONCE HUNTED (Book #5)
ONCE PINED (Book #6)
ONCE FORSAKEN (Book #7)
ONCE COLD (Book #8)
ONCE STALKED (Book #9)
ONCE LOST (Book #10)
ONCE BURIED (Book #11)

ONCE BOUND (Book #12)
ONCE TRAPPED (Book #13)
ONCE DORMANT (Book #14)
ONCE SHUNNED (Book #15)
ONCE MISSED (Book #16)
ONCE CHOSEN (Book #17)

**MACKENZIE WHITE MYSTERY SERIES**
BEFORE HE KILLS (Book #1)
BEFORE HE SEES (Book #2)
BEFORE HE COVETS (Book #3)
BEFORE HE TAKES (Book #4)
BEFORE HE NEEDS (Book #5)
BEFORE HE FEELS (Book #6)
BEFORE HE SINS (Book #7)
BEFORE HE HUNTS (Book #8)
BEFORE HE PREYS (Book #9)
BEFORE HE LONGS (Book #10)
BEFORE HE LAPSES (Book #11)
BEFORE HE ENVIES (Book #12)
BEFORE HE STALKS (Book #13)
BEFORE HE HARMS (Book #14)

**AVERY BLACK MYSTERY SERIES**
CAUSE TO KILL (Book #1)
CAUSE TO RUN (Book #2)
CAUSE TO HIDE (Book #3)
CAUSE TO FEAR (Book #4)
CAUSE TO SAVE (Book #5)
CAUSE TO DREAD (Book #6)

**KERI LOCKE MYSTERY SERIES**
A TRACE OF DEATH (Book #1)
A TRACE OF MURDER (Book #2)
A TRACE OF VICE (Book #3)
A TRACE OF CRIME (Book #4)
A TRACE OF HOPE (Book #5)

# PROLOGUE

Kate Minnett had legal matters weighing heavy on her mind as she climbed out of her BMW, glancing briefly at the crimson flare of the setting sun, and headed to her front door.

In particular, the legalities surrounding death. Violent, tragic death, leaving a slew of loose ends in its wake.

She slung her laptop bag, heavy with legal files as well as her computer, over her shoulder as she approached the house. Its weight pulled down, tugging at the shoulder of her smart navy jacket. She eased her head to the right so her shiny bobbed hair was freed from the strap, which had been pulling at a few strands.

"The property owner was stabbed in a mugging in the city center, fiancée is not mentioned in the will. Ex-wife still stands to inherit."

Kate mused over the complications of her job in the estate and inheritance legal field as she approached the front door. This wasn't one of her current cases. It was a case from a neighboring city. Not Boston, where she lived, but Springfield. A different branch of the legal firm she worked for, but they all put their heads together on complex cases.

She hoped she'd be able to find the best outcome, but sometimes, following the letter of the law was harsh. Nobody expected to be stabbed and robbed at the age of forty when walking back to the parking garage after a late business meeting. Very few people kept their affairs in pristine order.

Preoccupied with the potential outcome of the case, she put her key in the lock.

She knew already what she would find inside. The smell of her house, a mixture of polished floorboards and potpourri from the bowl she kept in the hall. She liked a very clean home and was something of a neat freak. At any rate, that was what Chad, her ex-husband, had always called her, in the increasing number of fights they'd had before the divorce and his move out of state a few years ago.

Now she was alone and she liked it that way. It was easier, and work was busy enough that she didn't miss romance in her life. Well, truth be told, perhaps she did. Just a little. Maybe next month she'd sign up on the dating site again, take the plunge once more, trawl through the pool of men that, in the over-thirties market, seemed to consist of a disproportionate number of weirdos and married men looking for fun on the side.

When they found she was a lawyer, both types melted away.

"Maybe the following month," she admitted to herself, thinking of what it would take, and the weirdos she'd already encountered. "Maybe in the spring."

For now, it was time to get one of her prepackaged healthy meals into the microwave, put her feet up, and think about the case challenges. Do some work while she ate her dinner, and then relax for an hour or two before following the yoga video tutorial that she forced herself to do at least four times a week.

She opened the front door.

And gasped.

There was somebody there, inside her home, facing her. Someone. Inside her home?

And not just any someone. A man, immaculately dressed in a pinstriped business suit, a glossy tie, a red button-down shirt, and shiny shoes. Looking as if he'd just walked out of a top-level boardroom, with a laptop bag slung over his shoulder. He looked entirely relaxed as he stared at her, as if he had every right to be strolling around in her house.

She let out an audible gasp. Fast and urgent, her heart pounded in her throat.

This couldn't be happening. It was a nightmare, a weird dream. It had to be, right? What was this man doing in her home? Who was he?

Tall, strong, broad-shouldered. Not speaking, but now smiling slightly. A gleeful, terrible expression that told her no good could come of this.

Run, Kate's brain told her, surfacing from the deep waters of total shock. Run. This isn't a dream. And you need to get away. Fast.

She turned, crying out as her ankle twisted, the heavy weight of her laptop bag unbalancing her as her heel caught.

And then rough hands behind her yanked her back, and she felt tough, strong fingers on her throat, pressing on the sides, cutting off the blood supply. She tried her best to fight the touch, but she'd done no more than frantically claw at the sleeves of that pinstriped suit jacket before darkness rushed in.

*

Reality filtered back. Slowly, painfully. Her throat ached. Her head pounded with a muzzy feeling, as if it had been starved of oxygen. Her mind felt bludgeoned by what had happened.

What had happened?

Now she was lying on a bed, and she opened her eyes, staring in bewilderment.

There was the bedside lamp. Her bedside lamp, with its cream edging and oval shade. Was she in bed? Had this crazy guy, this mirror image of herself, taken her inside the house? Had it all been the weirdest kind of bad dream?

But beyond, things were different, disjointed.

The wall was wrong. Not her cream-colored wallpaper, but a whitewashed surface that was uneven and blotchy. Not her artwork on the wall.

She sat up, choking, her throat in agony, her heart accelerating. What was going on?

And then, a voice from behind her, coming through a gap in the wall where she saw some holes had been drilled.

"You're going to become who I was. You'll become the old me, the person I need to erase."

The voice was a man's. Hoarse, unsteady, but full of triumph. The man in the smart suit? This was him. Memories surged and she gasped.

"Help!" she cried out. Then, knowing that this situation was deadly, that the man was a psycho, she screamed as loudly as she could.

"Help! Somebody! If you can hear me, help me! Please!"

She screamed until her throat was sore. But there was only a resounding silence. She couldn't hear another human being. She didn't think there was anyone else around.

Except for him.

He was laughing softly now. Chuckling to himself, an evil sound.

"You'd better make yourself as comfortable as you can, because we've got some important work to do soon. I hope you like your setting. Do you feel ready?"

She drew in a shuddery breath through her hoarse throat, because of course he'd been inside her house, inside her room, seeing it. Watching her.

"Why are you doing this?" she asked.

"Because I need to," he replied simply, his voice husky with excitement. "I need to take what I was and throw it away. Like I said, erase it. You're going to help me do it, that's all."

He laughed again, the most unpleasant, threatening sound.

"And then what?" she asked. "Then what?"

He was silent for a while. She felt sick with worry at what he might say.

But he said nothing.

There was only quiet from beyond that wall, where he could see in and she could not see out and nobody at all could hear.

Looking around her prison frantically, for any sign of a way out, she guessed that was all the answer she needed.

# CHAPTER ONE

Cami Lark was strategizing, sitting cross-legged on her bed in her student digs, thinking frantically as she analyzed her options.

She didn't like to feel she was at a dead end, but that was the way she was feeling now.

She felt blocked at every turn in her search to find the truth about what had happened to her sister Jenna, who'd disappeared six years ago. Looking into her disappearance had triggered a recent slew of disastrous events. Maybe blocked was the wrong word, she decided. It was more like being walled in by danger.

Lifting a hand, she twined her fingers anxiously through her dark-dyed hair, on the side where it was long enough to do that. The other side was shaven. She liked the black hair better than the natural blond, and thought it suited her green eyes and the intricate dark lines of the tattoos on her skin.

She tugged at the hair as the timeline flashed back in her mind, the sequence of events setting itself logically in her mind. She liked logic. You didn't get to be a star student at MIT, about to take final exams in computer science, and probably graduate top of the class, without liking logic.

And at that moment, while she was piecing together things in her mind, her phone rang.

She jumped, distracted from her thoughts by the noise, even though she'd been expecting the call. It was Kieran, Ethan's younger brother.

"Hi, Kieran," she said.

"Hey, Cami." The voice was painfully familiar. It made her remember Ethan all over again. Then Kieran said something that surprised her. "I'm here. I'm walking into MIT now. You want a coffee?"

"I'll come down," she said, uncurling herself from the bed, closing her laptop, pocketing her phone, and rushing downstairs. She felt happy that Kieran was here, on campus—a place she'd only be living for a couple of weeks longer. It was comforting that he'd come here to see her personally to touch base.

There he was, walking toward her, holding two cups. He was so similar to Ethan. Same clean-cut, handsome features, same dark hair, same height and rangy breadth of his shoulders. And weirdly, she felt the same lift of her spirits on seeing him that she always had when she'd been around Ethan.

"You okay?" He gave her a cup.

"Some days are better than others. Are you?" she replied.

"Getting there," he admitted.

Then he surprised her by giving her an awkward hug, even clumsier than it might otherwise have been because they were both holding coffees. But the hug was surprisingly warming. His strong arm around her felt good. Maybe it did to him, too. She'd lost a boyfriend she'd known for a couple of months and who'd meant the world to her, but Kieran had lost a brother who'd been part of his whole life.

"Shall we walk?" she asked, feeling restless, and also like she wanted to be far away from anyone while they talked. Plus, she'd been cooped up in her tiny room since the early hours, studying for her final exam.

"Sure," he said.

They set off, heading through the campus, to the sports fields beyond. Cami took a swallow of her coffee as they walked.

"I was going through everything in my head," she told him. "Trying to make sense of it all and make sure I have all the details correct. Right from the start of all of this. Up until the part you still don't know."

He glanced at her. "And? What have you figured out? And what don't I know?"

They headed down to the campus football field, treading along the perimeter of the mowed grass, which at this time of the day was still crisp with frost. Cami took another gulp of coffee, grateful for the warmth.

"This all started when my sister Jenna disappeared," she said, recapping for him. "That was six years ago. The FBI was called in and they didn't get anywhere. My dad, who's a cop, believed Jenna was a runaway, because she was a rebel."

"She was?" Kieran asked, emphasizing the word "she" as he glanced at Cami.

Cami was surprised to find herself grinning briefly at that. She liked Kieran's humor. "I guess we both were. Anyway, my dad didn't seem to think it was a problem that she'd gone. I knew she'd never have left.

Not my big sis. Not without saying goodbye. I didn't know what was happening in her life, but I knew she wouldn't do that."

"So the FBI got nowhere?"

"Correct," Cami said. "But then we fast-forward six years to when I got brought in to help the FBI with cases, after they caught me hacking their site."

"You know, Ethan told me about that," Kieran said, interrupting her story. "He came home and said he'd met this really pretty, rebellious woman who'd hacked the FBI's website, and everyone was mad about it, but that they'd given you a plea bargain because they were so short of IT talent in the Bureau. With agents getting lured away to work for startups."

"I'm glad he told you about it." Cami smiled, even though the pain of Ethan's loss still burned.

"Go on. I'm sorry, I thought I'd better mention it. In case you didn't know."

"Well, when I was able to access the FBI's databases, I looked up Jenna's file, and I discovered someone had put tracking software into Jenna's case file and deleted most of it."

"That's very significant," Kieran said. "That someone would have done that."

Cami nodded. "Anyway, I then found Liam Treverton had been in charge of the case, but he'd left the FBI under a cloud a few years ago. I managed to find out where he lived and get hold of his laptop."

Kieran gave her a sideways look, but didn't say anything.

"The laptop needed a voice recording to open it, so I worked out where Liam went in the evenings, and found out he sometimes visited this dodgy bar. When Ethan and I went to that bar, to get the voice recording to open his laptop, that's when the worst happened. We left, and someone followed us. Someone shot Ethan."

She glanced somberly at Kieran, who nodded, his face now grim.

"But then I found out from you that there had been trouble earlier. That someone had shot at Ethan before, out on the street near where you lived."

"Correct," Kieran said. "We thought it was some crazy guy terrorizing the neighborhood, or a criminal making a getaway. I had no idea it was anyone targeting Ethan. Not until this happened."

Cami nodded. They turned along the bottom of the field. Now, weak winter sunshine glowed, filtering down onto the frosty grass, making the icy crystals sparkle.

"So I am guessing that Ethan was also digging. He must have found out something was wrong. Maybe he'd stumbled across something that had raised red flags."

"Maybe," Kieran said.

"But someone else knew, too. Most likely, someone within the FBI."

"It's all pointing toward that," Kieran agreed.

"Jenna's case seemed to have been well investigated, at first," Cami said. "From what I saw on Liam's laptop, he didn't botch it. He did everything right. So down the line, either he was told to back off, or someone else stepped in."

"Yes. That's logical," Kieran said.

"So then I did something else," Cami said. "Something you don't know yet."

"What's that?" Kieran asked. Now there was a note of apprehension in his voice.

"I decided I was going to confront Liam about this," Cami said.

"What?" Kieran stopped in his tracks, turning to stare at her. "Confront him?"

"Yes. I figured it was the only way to get the information I needed. And that was where it got weird, because his reaction wasn't what I expected."

"What did he do?"

This was why Cami had wanted to be out in the open, far away from anyone, when she told Kieran this. Because right now, she didn't know who to trust. She remembered the expression in Liam's eyes, the fear in his voice.

"He said Jenna was a friend, he'd known her slightly before this happened. He said of course he didn't want to give the case up, but that he was forced to."

"Forced?" Kieran said. "That's so weird. That's not what I expected at all."

"Me, either. I asked who forced him. He wouldn't say. He said he wasn't getting involved in that again. That they are watching and they are listening."

Kieran's eyes widened as Cami continued.

"He said if I have any sense, I'll leave it be. He said…" Cami leaned closer. "He said, look what happened to Ethan. That this could happen to you or to me, and that maybe it would. He said I should drop it, keep my hands clean, not ask questions about Ethan, or about Jenna.

And that I shouldn't go digging into what happened to Jenna. Because it might get deadly."

She stared into Kieran's eyes, feeling a pang at how similar his gaze was to Ethan's, how she could see the same spark and the same emotion in his gaze.

"You think he was really scared? Or was he threatening you?"

"I think he was really scared," Cami said. "He wasn't threatening me, he was warning me. He was terrified. Basically, I'm getting the impression he left the FBI to save himself, and that he might have been forced into it, and he agreed just to get himself out of there and away. He got another very good job, I mean, he's not a deadbeat. He seems to be doing well. Nice house, nice car. He's clearly professional at what he does and I think he always was. Whatever happened at the FBI with him leaving, it wasn't because he was incompetent."

"I see what you mean," Kieran said. He stared at her, frowning. "This is serious, Cami. Because how do we know who to trust?"

"We don't know," she said. "And it's a problem, because there's one person I know I can trust—my boss, Connor, who partners with me when I come on board for FBI cases. But I can't tell him." She shook her head, feeling helpless.

"I get you," Kieran said. "You can't tell him because you don't know who else he'll have to tell. I mean, they've got a chain of command there, I guess. He can't keep things like that to himself."

"Exactly," Cami said. Whenever she thought about telling Connor, she felt two emotions. Utter relief at the thought of handing her problems over to someone she trusted. And then wretched fear, because she knew that he couldn't keep it private, and would have to share the information with others in the FBI. Others she didn't trust.

"I think we need to ask Liam more. I'll do it, if you like?" Kieran volunteered.

Cami felt a pang. No way. What if whoever was behind this targeted him too? She could see in his face that he wasn't going to let go of the idea.

"No. Please don't do that. Let me do it."

"But if you get face to face with him again, there's a big risk. A risk someone might see you, surely? And if you call him, and someone's keeping tabs? I know I'm maybe paranoid, but it seems he is too, and with reason," Kieran said, concern etched in his face.

Cami shook her head. "I don't have to get face to face with him. There's a way I can communicate without anyone knowing, and persuade him to tell us more. I've done it before, and I can do it again as soon as I'm back in my room."

# CHAPTER TWO

Kieran stared at Cami. She saw he now looked even more worried than he had a minute ago.

"What do you mean, Cami? What way are you going to try to get in touch with Liam?"

"I have his laptop," she explained. "I'm able to hack into some of his home's devices. I can set up a line of communication that way. It'll be a very discreet way of reaching out to him and requesting that we meet."

"I don't think you should do it alone," Kieran insisted. "If you meet up with him, I want to be there. It'll mean less risk for you, and also, what if he says something about Ethan that rings a bell for me?"

"I don't know." She looked at him dubiously. She did not want to put him at risk. And she had to accept that in these circumstances, doing this meant there was going to be danger.

"Ethan was my brother. I know Jenna was your sister—sorry, I didn't say that right. I mean, she is your sister," he said hurriedly, reddening in his confusion. "She's disappeared, not—not anything worse, that you know of. But I also need answers. Two heads are better than one, right? Especially since the FBI has Ethan's computer. They came to the house and took it a couple of weeks ago."

"They did?" Cami said, feeling appalled. "Who? Connor?"

"No. Someone else. I'm not sure who," Kieran said.

In all the shock of Ethan being shot and then fighting for his life in the ICU at a time when she was busy on a case with Connor, she hadn't thought about what would happen to his laptop. Only recently had she realized that there might be important information hidden away on it, and that Ethan might have been doing his own research, too.

What if the bad agents had taken it? Most likely they were going through that computer with a fine-tooth comb.

Were there any messages between her and Ethan on that laptop? She was pretty sure there were, and if they read them, they would see that there had been more between her and Ethan than just a working relationship.

That would mean the shooter who'd come after Ethan that night might now know who she was.

"What about his phone?" He'd organized everything on his phone. Their dates, their drinks. The outings that she couldn't think about now without a painful pang of grief.

"They took that too, a while ago. It wasn't until later that they came back for the laptop," he said.

Cami's gut twisted. With the phone, they would definitely know who she was. Even the arrangements for that night when he'd been shot were on the phone.

Maybe it had fallen into good hands, and the bad guys hadn't gotten hold of it, she hoped, but she knew she couldn't rely on that being the truth.

"We have to be careful," Cami said, her voice low. "I don't want to put you in more danger, Kieran. I won't forgive myself if anything happens to you."

"I can take care of myself," Kieran said, his voice firm. "And I won't let anything happen to you either. We have to do this, Cami. For Ethan, for Jenna, for ourselves."

Cami hesitated. Kieran was right, she needed someone else to help her, especially someone she could trust. And she could trust Kieran, she knew that. But the risk was still there, and she worried about what would happen if they got caught. This wasn't just a case of getting into trouble. This was a case of getting dead.

"Yes, two heads are better than one," she agreed. "But I also need to check with Liam. He was scared. He might not want to speak to anyone else. And if he clams up and won't say anything, that's a worst-case scenario."

"Okay. I see that. But if he is willing to, will you keep me in the loop?"

"I will."

They walked on, in step with each other. It was weird to feel this closeness with Kieran. He was so much the same kind of person Ethan had been. She got the impression the brothers, just two years apart in age, had shared a lot. The same sharp intelligence, the same quirky humor that she saw flashes of in both. And she could clearly see that Kieran had the same integrity and the same desire to find out the truth.

"I'll try to set something up," she said. She'd make sure it wasn't traceable. She'd use the dark web. She would not let this backfire on her.

Even though Cami knew it might already have. Whoever was on the other side might even now be trying to find out who the woman was who'd run down the street with Ethan on the night he was shot, and who'd hidden away from the gunman.

That search might lead them to her.

It filled her with cold fear, but paralyzing as that feeling was, she knew she had to fight it.

They were approaching the campus buildings again. Cami tossed her coffee in the trash, and Kieran did the same.

"It was nice seeing you," she said.

"Likewise," he agreed. Then he added, stammering slightly, "I know this might seem—well, it might seem weird. But I'd like to—when this is over, I mean, when we have some closure—I'd like to go out for a drink with you. As friends, I mean."

He wasn't doing this well, and he was blushing again, Cami saw in surprise. But she was even more astounded to realize that she wanted to go for a drink with him. She wanted to see him socially. There was something about him that she instinctively felt drawn toward.

"Sure," she said, and saw his face instantly warm.

"Good. That's great. I'm—I'm looking forward to it."

"Yeah, me too. But let's get over these other hurdles first," she warned.

"Let's do that. Whatever I can do to help, I will. Okay?"

"Okay. Stay safe, and I'll let you know."

He squeezed her hand briefly. Cami squeezed his in turn.

Cami felt a mix of emotions as she walked away. She was relieved to have an ally, and she felt a deepening of her connection with Kieran. She didn't know where this would lead, but she wasn't going to turn away from it. At the same time, though, she was scared to involve someone else in this dangerous game. Whoever had shot Ethan hadn't just disappeared off the face of the earth. The opposite was true. They were now going to be watchful, making their plans just as she was doing. That person, or more than one person, was still there, lurking in the shadows, waiting to pounce. She had to be vigilant, and she had to be careful.

And then, to complicate matters, there was the unexpected spark of emotion she felt toward Kieran, which made a place in her heart, a place that had felt frozen, warm up again.

Now, how to contact Liam discreetly?

The best way would be through his smart home command console, she decided. She was pretty sure that if she chose the right way of doing this, then only he would be able to get the message.

She'd hacked into his alarm system previously. But maybe an even better way would be to simply text him a message on the console.

Cami pulled out her phone and opened the hacking app, carefully selecting the right codes to bypass Liam's security measures. After a few moments of typing, she was inside his smart home system. It wasn't difficult because she'd done it before. And weirdly, he hadn't updated his passwords. Cami thought about that for a while.

Perhaps he'd left them unchanged purposely, and that meant he was open to communication with her and wasn't locking her out. At any rate, that was what she read into it.

She navigated through the menus until she found the console, then composed a message.

"I want to meet with u. Regarding J. And E. Time, place?"

She thought that was vague enough that if anyone did see it they wouldn't connect the dots, but that Liam would know instantly.

Taking a deep breath, Cami pressed Send.

Now the message would be visible on his command console, and she'd need to look into it again to see if he'd replied. He might take hours to do that. Days. It depended on how his alerts were set up.

She swallowed, hoping he would see it soon, knowing she was in uncharted waters here and that whoever these people were, they were playing for keeps. She was scared, too, and now she'd gotten a taste of exactly how scared Liam must be, the fear he'd been living with.

And then her phone rang again. Quickly, she took the call, seeing that it was her boss, Connor, from the FBI on the line.

Cami knew what that meant.

Another serious crime had been committed, and they needed her tech expertise on board to try to solve it.

# CHAPTER THREE

"Hello, Connor," Cami said. She did her best to sound normal. She didn't want to alert Connor that anything was wrong in her life. Otherwise he'd ask about it, and right now, she was scared to talk.

Luckily, he sounded distracted.

"Cami. You got a free day today?" he asked. As he spoke, she visualized him in her mind. She'd perceived him at first as a resented father figure, with his strong-jawed, serious face and his short dark hair, threaded with gray. It was only after a few fireworks between them that she'd acknowledged his wisdom, that he was a valuable mentor with a wealth of experience that backed up and complemented her tech expertise.

"Yes. I've been studying since five this morning, so I'm up to date, and my next exam's not until next week," she said.

"We've got an issue here that I'd like your help with."

"Sure. Gladly," she said. "What is it?"

As she spoke, Cami felt amazed by how far she'd come. When this "arrangement" to be on call to the FBI for tech-related cases had started, she'd been filled with anger and rebellion. Her grudge toward the FBI had originated with her sister's disappearance, when she felt they hadn't done enough to find Jenna. Being forced to help with tech-related cases for a year, as an alternative to a jail term for hacking their site, hadn't made her like them any better.

Now, with a few cases behind her, Cami was realizing what it took in terms of bravery, know-how, and sheer determination to catch people who were truly evil and had their own terrible agendas. Ethan had been the first person to change her mind about the FBI, when she'd realized how focused he was on his job, how supportive he was of his team, how determined he was to catch the bad guys.

And she'd grown to admire Connor. He was one of the toughest, most ethical people she knew. Tech wasn't his strong point, but people were, and she'd picked up a lot of wisdom on that front when watching him interact.

Now, she felt eager to help where she could, hoping that her input could help Connor and his team defeat this latest threat.

"We've had two women who have been found, strangled, and dumped in different parts of Boston," Connor said, and she could hear the regret in his voice. "The first body was found two days ago, the second, late last night. Police suspect it's a serial because the MO is so similar, but there's no obvious connection between the women. So we're looking to technology to give us a lead on that, and see if there's anything to be found," he explained.

Cami listened intently, her mind already whirring with ideas on how she could help.

"What's the first step?" she asked, eager to get started. "Do you have any of their devices?"

"We've got both the victims' phones. Their phones and personal items were on them, although the phones were turned off, and they've been taken into evidence. Both are at the local police stations where the crimes were called in, but we're organizing for the first phone to be transferred to the second police station in central Boston. So, if you're ready, I can pick you up in fifteen minutes."

"I'll be ready," Cami said.

*

Fifteen minutes later to the minute, Cami saw the plain gray Ford that Connor was using as his unmarked speed around the corner in the direction of the university entrance. She rushed to the car as it pulled up and jumped inside.

"Thanks for coming on board with this, Cami," Connor said as he hit the gas, pulling away from the curb. "With a potential serial case, you know how important it is to get onto it fast. It's a very troubling set of circumstances, and the two victims are very different. No clear links between them."

Cami nodded. "I hope I can find something," she said.

At the start of a case, she couldn't help feeling intimidated by the sheer amount of information they needed to find. It was like staring at a blank computer screen that needed to be filled with specialized coding before the program could run. That was what she compared it to in her mind. At the same time, she was proud of being so valued by Connor. Her hacking ability could sometimes provide the key to solving cases that might otherwise remain unsolved. And she could usually get information far quicker, and also more of it, than the FBI could otherwise get. The fact she sometimes did so through "alternative" channels was her strength.

As they neared the first police station, weaving through the heavy morning traffic, Connor briefed her on the details they had so far.

"The most recent victim is an estate lawyer named Kate Minnett, age thirty-three. She lived alone in a quiet residential suburb west of downtown. Low crime area, wealthy residents, and as you can imagine, this is causing a major outcry."

"What's the timeline on that?" Cami asked.

"She left the office on Wednesday evening at about five p.m. Her home's half an hour away from the office. Then she didn't respond to a call from her boss at six p.m., her phone was off, and she wasn't in the office yesterday. So that narrows the timeline down as to when she was taken. She had said she'd keep her phone on."

"Okay," Cami said, taking this in as Connor continued.

"Two of the law firm's partners went around yesterday evening to check she was okay. Her house was unlocked, her laptop bag was inside the front door, and she was gone. Her body was found in a dumpster late last night." Connor paused, then added in a heavy voice, "The police interviewed her work colleagues yesterday evening, and everyone's horrified. She was well liked, there was no motive for the crime, she hadn't complained of anything unusual. And of course, they then linked it to the other crime, which took place a couple of days earlier and on the other side of the city."

"And details on the other?" Cami asked, feeling a chill of horror at the circumstances. Nobody should be able to get away with doing that. Not even once, never mind twice. And if she could stop the tragedy from occurring again, then she'd do whatever it took.

"The other victim was a younger woman, age twenty-three, who lived in a small apartment in a new housing estate a few miles from the city center. She worked at a local beauty salon doing nails. Her name's Gracie Foster. She disappeared sometime over the weekend, although the timeline's not clear. She worked Saturday morning at the salon, and was then supposed to be in again on Monday. She wasn't, and her body was found early Tuesday morning. Also in a dumpster, and probably placed there during the night."

"Any problems in her life, any boyfriend issues?" Cami knew from experience that those were important and could be an initial lead.

"No. Both these women lived alone, with no romantic ties, no close family nearby," Connor said.

"Any sign of forced entry?" she asked, wondering if the victims had lived in smart homes, and if that was how the killer had gotten access.

"There are possible signs. Gracie's kitchen door latch was loose, and it could have been forced and then roughly repaired. There was a window in Kate's living room with some marks on the frame that also looked as if it might have been pried open and then closed again. So, yes. Someone could have gotten in through the weak points of both homes and waited inside."

Not smart homes. The opposite. But a smart killer, for sure, who'd taken advantage of gaps in the defenses, Cami knew.

Connor peeled off the stop-start traffic on the main road, powering down a side street that quickly led to the police station. He climbed out, and Cami grabbed her laptop bag and followed him.

He headed inside.

"Agent Connor, FBI, and Cami Lark, tech expert," he introduced them. "It's regarding the double murder. I believe both the victims' phones are available here?"

The officer glanced at a checklist. "Yes, Agent. The second phone arrived half an hour ago. The laptop for Kate Minnett is also in evidence if you want it. We're short on space, but there's a mini office just outside the evidence room that you can use. I'll get the phones signed out and available for you."

Already, Cami was priming herself in her mind, making a mental checklist of the programs she might need to access the phones. She followed Connor through the labyrinth of corridors, to the back office that adjoined the locked steel door of the evidence room.

They went inside the tiny office, which barely had space for a desk and two chairs. But at least it was warm and cozy and it had a couple of plug points.

As she waited, Cami heard the regular clanging of the steel door and the beeping of a keypad as authorized people accessed the evidence room in this busy police station.

"Here are the phones and the laptop." The officer brought them in, and Cami set them up, getting them on chargers and taking a look at both phones. One Android, one iPhone. One old, one brand new. One had certain security features she knew her program could bypass in an hour, and the other had a manufacturing flaw that her online hacking group had found out about. The laptop was a MacBook Pro.

“I can get into both phones, hopefully, as well as the laptop. Maybe in an hour,” she said, setting up her program to run, plugging the devices in so that they each connected with one of hers.

While the program ran, Cami got onto social media to learn more about Kate Minnett and Gracie Foster. She wanted to get an idea of the personalities, interactions, issues, and connections that they displayed to the world—or at least, to their friends.

And while she was doing that, she listened to Connor’s voice as he took a call with the coroner.

“Strangulation the cause of death in both cases?” he asked, jotting notes on an old-fashioned paper notepad that she knew was how he preferred to work. “And any DNA?”

He waited and jotted some more, muttering the details to himself. “Both moved after death. How long after? A couple of hours. Okay. And signs of a struggle?”

The pen scribbled inexorably over the paper. “In both cases, yes. Defensive wounds. And torn nails, bruises.” He paused. “Reckon they were locked away somewhere?” He paused and listened again.

It was horrific to have to imagine what these victims had endured, but Cami was only hearing it with part of her mind. The rest was taking note of the women’s social interactions, which she was researching while waiting for her hacking program to run. Neither of them had a very public or visible online profile, and Kate’s profile seemed to be purely focused on business. Neither one lived their life on social media, with every action publicly announced. Both were fairly private. Neither could have been stalked based on their online interactions.

That ruled out a few of the most obvious conclusions, straight up. So, what else could she find?

At that moment, Cami’s computer beeped.

She’d gotten into Kate’s phone faster than she’d thought. That manufacturer’s flaw that her hacking group had detected was easy to bypass. That meant she could get into the laptop more easily, too. Another few moments, and she had access to that.

“I’m in Kate’s devices,” she said. And then the other phone beeped, too. “I’m in both.”

Now totally focused on her job, and shutting out Connor’s conversation completely, Cami began hunting, seeking out the contacts and the messages, setting new searches to run, looking for any connections that these two women might have had in common. That was the first and most important lead, a person in common. A friend, an ex-boyfriend, a work colleague, an insurance salesman—she'd learned that a killer could hide in any guise.

She scanned the list with narrowed eyes, looking carefully, double-checking herself as her programs sped along in the background. There were many more contacts in Kate's phone. She had a massive network of work colleagues, but also a large number of private friends. Gracie had far fewer.

Almost immediately, Cami ruled out the laptop. It had been used purely for work. It was a few months old and there wasn't a single social message or email on it. This was simply for recording progress on cases and networking with colleagues about work-related issues. Cami got the impression that Kate was a very disciplined woman. If there was another side to her personality or her interactions, it would have to be found on the phone.

A quick look at the phones showed her what she was sure the police had already checked. No trouble, no fights, no angry messages, no breakups. No obvious signs that the women were in trouble with anyone, or that anything was amiss in their lives. Kate had sent work texts earlier in the day. Gracie had made vague plans to meet up with a group of friends she seemed to see monthly.

Anyone in common? She'd set the search, although she didn't feel hopeful about the results. But as her phone beeped yet again, Cami felt her heart speed up.

She'd gotten the unexpected. A mutual contact.

"They do have someone in common," she said to Connor, surprised. "And if you give me a minute, I'll tell you who they are."

# CHAPTER FOUR

The name Maxwell Reed had come up immediately in the contacts of both women, and the same phone number had pinged Cami's programs and drawn her gaze simultaneously. Two seemingly unrelated women both knew this man well enough for him to be in their phone contacts? Cami thought that was a massive clue.

Trawling further into the records, she saw that they'd both connected with him recently.

"Who is he?" Connor asked her eagerly.

"His name is Maxwell Reed," she told Connor. "He's had phone calls with Kate Minnett and Gracie Foster recently."

"And what does Mr. Reed do?" Connor inquired.

"According to his listing here, he's a professional counselor," she said. "He specializes in health and wellness coaching."

"So you think he would have seen both women? Clients, maybe?"

"Yes, it would seem so," Cami confirmed. "The phone calls from Kate and Gracie were made to his work number. And there are calls from his work number back to them again. I would guess that means he did see them both."

"As clients." Connor sounded thoughtful.

"It definitely looks that way," Cami said, scrolling through the call logs.

"You've found an important lead there. We need to talk to this counselor, Maxwell Reed, right away. Can you find his address easily?"

"There's a business address here. I'm not sure where he lives," she said.

"That, I can look up," Connor said. He looked stern as he closed his notepad, which was filled with jotted notes, details on the autopsy and on those defensive wounds. She felt relieved to have not really been listening. Thankfully she'd been too focused on pinpointing the contacts.

"Okay. So I see here, from what you've found, that his consulting office is about halfway between the two women's home addresses. And in this database, I'm seeing he lives a few miles away. Again, central."

His voice was meaningful. "It looks like he moved there four years ago. What's his history, I wonder?"

Gathering more information before they set out, Connor sent his fingers clacking over the keys.

Cami felt a quick, affectionate smile warm her face as she listened to the pace of his typing. She'd know Connor's rhythm if she was blindfolded. Slow and deliberate, that was him. It wasn't the rapid machine gun fire that the programmers at MIT did, without even a glance at the keyboard.

And yet, slow as he might be, Connor got results. Like now.

He looked over at Cami, an eyebrow raised. "Now, this is interesting," he said.

"What is?" She leaned sideways to take a look at the screen. "I don't understand. What am I seeing?"

"It's what we're not seeing," Connor explained.

"And what's that?"

"Any past history. It's like this ID record just popped into life four years ago. There's something strange about that. It either means it's been changed or corrupted along the way, or else, it's new."

"New?" Cami raised her eyebrows.

"Yup. Might have changed his name, moved from another state. For that, we'd need to go into a different database. It might be a red flag, and he could be a fake. Either way, we need to check it out, and I'm going to put my office onto that while we get going. We need to find out if he's legit, and if he saw these women."

Cami felt enthused. Leaving the phones in the office, Connor strode out, waiting for Cami to leave and then locking the office behind them.

As he headed out of the police station, he was on the phone to the FBI office. A month ago, Cami knew with a pang, Ethan would have been his go-to there. Now, she didn't know who he was speaking to. Perhaps she didn't want to know. Nobody could fill those shoes, ever. Nobody.

"I want a background check on the health counselor Maxwell Reed." He read out the address. "There's something strange about the record. It's not going back as far as it should, and I want to know why." He paused. "Great. Thanks."

Then he strode to the car, with Cami hurrying alongside. This case was already exposing potential irregularities. She felt optimistic that the killer had been careless, and that this would allow them to find the common thread between the victims.

Reed was hiding something. At any rate, she suspected it. And two women were dead.

"I heard you saying, on the phone, that the bodies were moved. Do you know anything about where they were held? Is there anything we need to look out for at his premises? Or his home?" Cami asked.

"Nope. At this stage there's nothing helpful, but the pathologist will look for more when he does the postmortem. But so far, knowing they were held, and moved after death, does give us some parameters."

Connor swerved to the left, pulling into the fast lane.

"Yes," Cami said. "It means this guy—I'm guessing a guy—is strong enough to be able to carry women, he has a place to keep them where other people can't hear, he has a car to transport them in." Cami checked off the points on her fingers, causing Connor to give her an approving glance.

"Yup. You've got it."

There was cohesion between them. Cami felt pleased about that. It had taken a while. She and Connor couldn't have gotten off on a worse footing to start with. She thought back to those conflicted hours they'd spent together, each one resenting the other. And now look at them. They were partners who were on each other's wavelength.

Or so Cami thought until Connor cleared his throat, and in a different tone of voice, spoke again.

"So. While we're driving, tell me this."

She stared at him, suddenly apprehensive.

"Tell you what?"

"Tell me what you're doing, looking into Ethan's death and opening old case files," he said. "I hear you've been banging on doors and upending trashcans. Figuratively, at least. What's going on?"

The words were like a hammer blow. Cami literally gasped. Her heart sped up and her mind was racing. How did he know? How had he found out exactly what she was doing?

"I'm—I'm not," she stammered. It was a weak, flimsy automatic denial and she knew it wouldn't wash with him. It didn't, of course. In between glancing ahead at the traffic, Connor seemed to be pinning her with his gaze in a way she couldn't escape.

"I don't want lies," he said firmly.

Cami swallowed hard, buckling under the gravity of the situation. She had tried to be so careful, and although she had spoken to Liam Treverton, he'd been scared, too. He hadn't seemed like a man who'd run straight back to the FBI and tell them what had happened. Had someone seen that she'd opened Jenna's case file? Had it alerted the wrong person? Was that even what Connor was referring to? She guessed he was being deliberately vague, waiting for her to supply the details.

She couldn't tell Connor. Especially since some of what she'd done had been outside the law. She didn't want Connor to know, or to be involved, because that would mean he'd tell others, and not only would it then cause trouble for Cami, but someone he told might be the shooter. She doubted Connor knew all his associates well enough to know whether it was or wasn't them. If he passed this on, it might end up going to unknown people.

"I'm just trying to understand what happened," she said carefully. "I need closure. I'm just asking a few questions."

He shook his head. "That's not what I heard," he said.

Cami's heart was pounding in her chest. She knew she had to choose her words carefully, or she could end up completely destroying the trust between them, making a bad situation worse. She swallowed hard, trying to come up with a coherent response which, at the same time, wouldn't bury her.

"What do you mean? Who told you?" she asked, hoping to buy herself some time.

Connor glanced at her before he focused back on the road.

"I was told in confidence," he said. "And the person who told me also said that if you go digging, you'll be opening up a can of worms and putting yourself at risk. So I want to know—what are you doing? What have you found? And I'm not going to take no for an answer here. Not when your safety is an issue."

His voice sounded as hard as she'd ever heard it.

Nothing could save her now. Connor was like a bulldog when it came to pursuing things like this. He wasn't going to drop it. He was not going to forget it. The most she could hope for was a temporary reprieve.

And she might have one—for now, at least, because Connor was turning into the street where Maxwell had his office.

"Oh look, is that Maxwell's place ahead?" she said in a wobbly voice. "Shouldn't we hurry there?"

"I'm not forgetting this," Connor threatened. "Questioning this suspect takes priority now. But by the end of today, Cami, I want to know."

He climbed out of the car and strode toward the office block, leaving Cami scrambling to follow, her hands damp and her stomach twisting with foreboding.

She was in so much trouble. And if she told him the truth, more would follow.

# CHAPTER FIVE

"Dance for me."

His voice was husky. His eyes were fixed on the gap in the wall, from where he could see her bedroom. Or rather, the bedroom he'd made for her. Because it was not the same, although he'd added similar items. For his last victim, a lamp provided the common factor. For this one, he'd found an identical set of scatter cushions, and exactly the same rug in front of the bed.

Now she was sitting, hunched on the bed, looking terrified. Looking for a way out that she wouldn't find, because there wasn't one.

"Dance for me," he pressured her. She'd arrived home late, dressed in a brightly colored smock. He'd done his best to match his own clothing with her colorful personality, wearing a bright blue business suit, a yellow tie, and a crisp white shirt when he met her at the door. It was important to him that he—or rather, the new him—dovetailed with his victims' personalities.

Maybe that was why he was angry with her now. He'd tried so hard, and now she should have made it easier for him. Anger was always his weak point, the emotion he couldn't handle. But then, he guessed with a rueful grimace, that was a family trait all right.

She raised her head and stared in his direction. He saw panic flare in her eyes. Yet again, he was glad he'd thoroughly tested the soundproofing of this home, a couple hundred yards from the nearest buildings on a large acreage, and those buildings were old stables, now used to house farm machinery. The stable block further muffled the noise, preventing it from reaching the nearest house, another couple hundred yards away.

She pushed back her curly brown hair and he grinned. Not panic. She was making a weak attempt at defying him. This was going to be a battle—with an invisible adversary, since she couldn't see him.

"I'm not dancing for you. Let me out," she said.

"Dance for me!" he insisted. He wanted to see her dance. When he'd watched her through the window last night, she'd been dancing alone in her living room. It hadn't been for joy. He'd thought she was practicing some steps for the Latin American dancing class she took, but it had still been intriguing, enrapturing even, and he'd absorbed the sight with greedy eyes.

"Please, I can't do this," she pleaded, her voice shaking. "I refuse!"

He frowned. He didn't like when they didn't comply.

"I said dance," he growled. "And you'd better do what I say. There is no room for negotiation. Not any at all."

Slowly, she stood up and began to move. Her body was rigid with fear, but she was doing her best to comply with his twisted request. He watched her every move, his eyes gleaming with pleasure. It wasn't the dancing that he loved. It was the fact that he was making her do it. He was removing her from her world.

Watching her, waiting for the moment when she'd have to wear those old, shabby clothes, he felt as if he was about to leave the memories of his old life behind for good this time. For a moment, he was a different person. It was an intense surge of joy through him.

As she danced, he moved along with her, hidden from her sight. He wanted to feel every step she took, every move she made. He wanted to be as close to her as possible, to feel her fear and her pain. His heart was pounding in his chest with excitement. He felt alive, more than he had felt in years. This was his masterpiece, his project, his passion. And he wanted to enjoy every moment of it.

Even though she wasn't really dancing very well, but then, nor was he. He wasn't much of a dancer either, but it was the thought that mattered.

In any case, it was now time for the next step.

"You can stop," he said, and watched her. Like a puppet whose strings were cut, she collapsed down.

More to come. This was the next challenge he needed from her. It wasn't time for her to rest yet, although he knew she would rest soon. Her time was nearly done. But he craved more.

"Put on the clothes on the bed," he commanded her.

She looked toward him.

"The clothes?"

"Yes. The ones on the bed."

He'd left a different set of clothes. A set of scruffy old clothes more suited to a man. Plain jeans, a flannel shirt, heavy shoes. She needed to put those on, to step out of her life and to be the sad, struggling person he was long ago. It was a deeply symbolic gesture for him.

"I'm not putting those on," she said. "Dancing is one thing. But taking my clothes off and putting this on? Are you joking? Why should I do that?" Her voice was high. Shrill.

He felt his patience slipping away. This one was proving to be difficult. They always started out that way, but eventually, they all complied. He just had to be patient.

"You will do as I say," he warned her, his voice low and menacing. "Or you will suffer the consequences."

"The consequences?" she repeated, a note of fear creeping into her voice.

"I'm a violent man," he told her. He didn't want it to, but his voice rose to a shout. "I'm a violent man and I love what I do. I won't hesitate to hurt you. Don't make me! Don't make me!"

She stared at him, her eyes wide with fear. Tears glistened on her cheeks.

"Okay," she whispered, her voice trembling. "Okay, I'll do it. I'm doing it."

She reached for the clothes with shaking hands, her eyes never straying away from him.

For a moment, he felt a strange twinge of guilt. He pushed it aside quickly. What happened in his own past, the things he'd been forced to do long ago, need not trouble him now. He had moved past that and become his own person. And now she had to do as he said.

She did as ordered, slowly and shakily, her movements jerky and her eyes still wide with fear. She ripped off her clothing with her back to the wall with the holes, not that he was interested in her body. It meant nothing to him. It was her mind that he wanted to see, to sense. That was what gave him the flashbacks, and made him realize with a crumb of comfort that he was on the other side now. The winning one.

When she was done, he nodded.

"That's fine. No, no. Keep them on. Keep them on. You can rest now."

She sank down on the bed, wearing the man's clothes. He could see her shoulders shaking, her face a mess of tears.

"Rest," he said again, more softly this time. "We'll go soon."

She nodded and lay down, curling up into a ball as if to protect herself from the world.

Almost reluctantly, he moved away, leaving her alone with her thoughts and her tear-streaked face.

Deep within, he knew something wasn't right. What he had done was wrong, he knew that in his heart. But it was only what he'd experienced. All he was doing was passing it on. And at least he killed them afterward. After all, it would be so wrong to let them live in the same misery he'd done.

Ending their lives was doing them a favor.

He smiled as he thought about it, knowing that she couldn't see him from behind the small holes in that wall.

# CHAPTER SIX

As Connor lifted his hand to rap on Maxwell Reed's office door, he paused, his face changing. Cami felt instant tension fill her. Something was wrong. Had Connor picked up a red flag, or was this something even more serious?

Rushing up to stand beside him, Cami looked anxiously at the red brick building, with the window blinds and the planters outside, and the brass notice board next to the door advertising "Health & Diet Services."

Then she heard it, from inside.

A breathless, plaintive moaning noise that made her stomach tighten and sent adrenaline pumping through her.

"The hell?" Connor muttered.

Connor raised his hand and brought it down loudly, hammering on the door with a deafening bang. And then, without waiting for an answer, he turned the handle and shoved it hard.

The door wasn't locked. It burst open and Connor barged his way inside, into a small reception area with a tidy front desk that was unoccupied. A blue office chair was placed behind it, there was a vase of flowers on the desk, and there were a few framed posters on the wall of weight charts, nutrition profiles of fruits and vegetables, and the calorie-burning properties of various exercises.

But the moaning was coming from the door at the back, and it was here that Connor now headed purposefully. Cami could hear thuds and scuffling coming from beyond.

Connor flung his weight against this door. It was locked. He rattled the handle.

"FBI. Open up. Now!"

More scuffling, and then silence. Cami waited, her heart pounding.

Then the door flew open, and they were face to face with the man that she recognized from her research earlier.

Maxwell Reed's blue shirt collar was askew and the shirt itself was hanging out of his pants. His face, which had looked round in the photo but was slimmer in real life, was flushed and misted with perspiration.

His brown hair, cut in a trendy style with shorter sides and length on top, was mussed.

Cami was starting to realize what was going on here. The picture was made even clearer when she saw the woman behind him, on the long, navy couch, frantically tugging at her skirt and looking for her shoes.

Irregular activities had been taking place here, undoubtedly. Just not the ones they'd been hoping to find. But maybe those were still happening elsewhere.

Cami realized they might not be finding this out as easily as they'd hoped to. Because, at that moment, Maxwell himself made a leap for the window.

Cami gasped as he shoved it open and got his leg over the sill. Connor, showing a sudden turn of speed, dashed across the office and made a determined grab for the fleeing man.

He managed to get hold of Maxwell's arm at the last possible moment. Maxwell yelled, sounding angry and panicked. "Let go of me!"

"Get back in here!" Connor commanded.

A fist thudded against the window frame.

Cami stood, feeling conflicted. She should run to help, but she didn't know how effective she could be in this close-quarters fight. And then she realized there was something even more important she could do.

The woman had her shoes on and was eyeing the door.

Cami quickly moved to lock it. She slammed it, turned the latch, and stood in front of it, trying to look as authoritative as possible. No way was she going to let a witness leave.

"Get out of my way," the woman threatened breathlessly.

"No," Cami replied, standing her ground.

"I need to leave."

"Only after my boss has finished asking you some questions."

Cami glanced at the window, where Connor was now physically hauling Maxwell back inside, to the accompaniment of thumps and struggling sounds.

"Get out of my way." The brunette woman, eyes flashing, stepped forward and shoved Cami's shoulder.

Cami gasped as she was flung back against the door with a thudding sound. She didn't have a weapon on her; she didn't even have any real authority to stop the woman. And if it came to a struggle, this bigger, taller woman was going to win the day.

But there was one thing she could do to keep her at bay. One way she could prevent her from leaving while Connor wrestled with Maxwell.

Cami scrambled to regain her footing, standing squarely in front of the door again. Then she took her phone out of her pocket, quickly swiping it on.

"You go ahead then," she said. "Come at me. Try your best to get me out of the way. But if I press this button, then I'm going to start livestreaming what happens onto my social media, set to public, and then I'm going to share it on all the groups I can find, while explaining what I saw in here while we arrived. What work do you do? Would your workplace want this published? What about your family?"

The threat, though breathless and uttered in a squeaky voice, proved effective. The woman flinched away, looking horrified.

"Don't you dare press that button," she hissed, making a grab for Cami's arm, but this time, Cami was too quick. She leaped out of her way, still clutching the phone.

"I'm filming unless you sit down," Cami said. "Footage starting in three… two… one…"

At the word "one," the woman turned, flounced over to the couch, and angrily seated herself on it, keeping her face turned away from Cami's phone.

The struggle at the window was abating. Connor had hauled Maxwell back inside. Now he clipped a set of handcuffs onto his wrist, affixing the other end to the arm of the visitor's chair.

"Sit," Connor commanded, and Maxwell thudded down into the chair.

Now that his escape attempt had been curbed, he was going for affronted innocence, Cami saw.

"What's going on here?" he asked in breathless tones, staring at Connor and then at Cami with an incredulous expression in his pale blue eyes. "How can you just—just barge in like this? Abuse me? Handcuff me?"

"We have questions for you," Connor said sternly. "Is this your client? What's your relationship with this woman?"

Seeing the woman's lips pressed together, Cami thought she might be regretting her life decisions. Particularly the last few recent ones. But to Cami, she didn't look as if she was here against her will. She couldn't see any evidence of that. The woman looked embarrassed, but not traumatized. And the way she'd tried to leave had been bossy and entitled, but not as if she was scared and needing to flee the area.

"My client," Maxwell said, reddening.

"Are you here of your own volition?" Connor demanded of the woman.

She nodded, still not speaking.

"What are you doing here, exactly?" Connor pressed.

Maxwell shifted from foot to foot, looking guilty. "Just consulting, you know. Nutritional advice. That kind of thing."

Well, that was the first lie out of the way, Cami thought. Even with a wealth of evidence to the contrary, Maxwell was doggedly pursuing the story of innocence. But where there was one lie, there might be others. A man sleeping with clients in his consulting office—after a strange name change somewhere in his past—might be committing serious crimes on the side.

"Ma'am, give me your ID," Connor commanded.

"Why?" the woman asked defensively, her first word to Connor so far.

"I need to check it," Connor said.

She stared at him mutinously. Then she picked up her purse from the floor, rummaged inside it, and handed him her driver's license.

Connor photographed it with his phone.

"Ursula Southbridge?"

"That's me," she said, tightening a hair grip in her thick, brown hair that had come loose.

"You are here of your own free will?"

"I am." She raised her chin defiantly. "I—we were working through some issues and Maxwell was comforting me."

"I see. You've had other sessions in the past, Ms. Southbridge?"

Maxwell, sitting handcuffed to the chair, began blurting something out, but Connor held up a hand. "I'm talking to the lady."

"This was my third session," she said.

"The others were?"

"I have one a month."

"So you've been here once a month for three months?"

"Yes."

"Seen or heard anything untoward in that time? Anything suspicious take place in those sessions?"

"No! Our sessions are very private. Usually," she said, narrowing her eyes and directing an angry stare at Connor.

He sighed. "Okay, ma'am. We may need to contact you again, but for now, you can go."

She stood and flounced out, a picture of irate embarrassment.

"Now," Connor said, turning to Maxwell. "Your ID, Mr. Reed?"

His flushed face went a few shades darker.

"What about my ID?" he stammered defensively.

"It appears to be fake."

"I—no, it isn't. I changed my name. Five years ago, after an acrimonious divorce. My ex was trashing my reputation. I wanted to make a fresh start, that's all. So I moved from Minnesota and came here."

Cami had no doubt there were two sides to that story. She didn't think Maxwell was an innocent party in any way. And she didn't even know if she trusted his story.

"Your license? To practice?"

"I don't need one," he shot back defiantly. "I'm an advisor, not a licensed professional. I've done an online course."

Connor sighed. "Do you know Kate Minnett and Gracie Foster? I believe they used your services?" He emphasized the word "services," and Maxwell shuffled his feet.

"Client confidentiality prevents me talking about this."

"You just said you're not a licensed professional," Connor shot back. "Plus, both these women are dead."

"What?" Now, Maxwell's eyes and mouth flew wide. "Dead?"

"Both murdered in the last couple of days," Connor said.

"I—I had no idea. I heard something about a murder on the news, I think, but didn't take note of it." Now his defiance was melting away. "I thought you were just here to cause trouble for me, that my ex-wife or someone's husband had set you on me."

"You understand it's more serious than that now?"

"Yes, I understand." He paused, as if gathering himself. "I'm ready to answer the questions now."

"Tell me about your interaction with Kate Minnett," Connor said.

Watching this play out, Cami was starting to wonder if this was their suspect. He'd appeared so genuinely shocked to hear about the deaths. He could be an excellent liar, but she wasn't sure he was that good at it.

"I counseled Kate a while back. She's a very busy lawyer and wanted to make healthier food choices. I helped her in that regard," he said, now with a hint of self-satisfaction in his voice. "Gave her meal plans and menu ideas. She was very happy. We were in touch a few weeks ago for a follow-up."

"And Gracie Foster?"

"That name's not familiar," he said. "I haven't seen her as a client. But I do presentations to small businesses, helping them make better food choices for slimness and health. I've done a few of those in the last month or two. She could have attended that, and if so I would have called her to follow up, and she might have returned the call if she was busy. Does she work in the hair and beauty industry? I've done a few presentations to small businesses in hairdressing and aesthetics in the last few months."

Cami didn't think this was a lie. It sounded plausible. And Gracie was a beautician.

"Your movements last night?" Connor asked. "In particular, from around five to seven p.m."

Now Maxwell was cooperating in a surprisingly willing way. The news of the murders seemed to have jolted him severely.

"Yesterday, I was at the Health Symposium in town, gaining further knowledge in a nutrition class. I was in class the whole afternoon, and I signed out at six p.m. and picked up my daughter from an art class on the way home. She's sixteen, and she stays with me for her vacations," he said anxiously.

"And then?"

"Then we drove home, via a pizza restaurant. Got home at about nine p.m."

That wasn't a healthy food choice, Cami thought, noting the incongruity between what Maxwell practiced and what he preached.

"Your street has cameras? Your house?"

"Yes, it does." Maxwell nodded energetically.

"I need to see that footage."

"I'll arrange it for you."

"Now!" Connor's tone brooked no argument.

While Maxwell got on the phone, Connor's phone also rang and he began speaking in low, rapid tones.

By the time he'd finished his conversation, Maxwell had produced the confirmation of him leaving the course, as well as the pizza receipt and the footage which showed his car arriving home just after nine p.m.

It drove into the garage and didn't leave again until the following morning. Cami checked the time stamps carefully as the footage scrolled past.

"Okay," Connor said. "You're cleared. Of this."

He stared dubiously at Maxwell and Cami knew he didn't fully believe the "fresh start" story, but didn't have time to pursue it further, with the pressure of this case taking priority.

As he walked out, he said to Cami, "That was the pathologist calling. He's done the postmortem on Kate Minnett. He needs to see us urgently, because he's got findings that may shed light on how and where the victims were held."

## CHAPTER SEVEN

Bodies held secrets, and Cami knew they needed to know what those were.

But immediately after Connor said the word "postmortem," her stomach started churning. This was her least favorite part of the cases she was involved in. She always felt a deep sense of relief when she didn't have to attend one. They really traumatized her, even though she knew that Connor wouldn't force her to go to one unnecessarily.

It was because of Jenna, and the unknowns surrounding her sister. Seeing a body lying on that steel table brought all her fears to the surface. It forced her to confront the terrible truth that Jenna might be dead.

Cami remembered the argument she'd had with Connor the first time they'd gone to the pathology lab, and the way she'd shut down.

Now, she felt determined that she was going to see this damned thing through, and she was not going to show how much it disturbed her. And furthermore, she promised herself, she was going to find a clue. She was going to prove herself and add value, even if she couldn't do it through her hacking skills in that environment.

"Let's go, then," she said, through gritted teeth.

She knew Connor hadn't forgotten about what he wanted to ask her. About Ethan. But she guessed that since they were on the way to discuss autopsy results, he was cutting her some slack.

"Pathologist's offices aren't too far away," he said, glancing at the main road as he strode to the car. "Further out of town. We'll be going against the traffic. Should get there in ten minutes."

Cami nodded and followed him to the car, the knot in her stomach growing tighter with each passing moment. She climbed into the car and breathed deeply, trying to calm herself, even though she already felt her anxiety surging.

The drive took less than ten minutes. The area where Maxwell's office was located, consisting of small homes and offices, changed to a suburban area of larger homes with treed yards. And then, veering down a side street, Connor headed out of this pretty suburbia and into a starker area of light industrial buildings and warehouses. Ahead, a small, official-looking signboard on the steel fence advertised the pathologist's office.

It was a grim-looking building that seemed to cling to the ground, painted in gray, with a high gate protecting it. The guard checked Connor's ID before opening the gate and directing him to a parking lot on the side. Several vehicles and two coroner's vans were already parked there. Cami took another deep breath as she saw them. The deep breathing wasn't working so well right now, but she persisted.

As they entered the building, Cami breathed in the smell of disinfectant that was so strong it burned her nostrils. She shook her head, trying to clear it, and focused on following Connor into the building. Inside, the stark, sterile environment didn't ease her anxiety. The hallway was white, with a gray tiled floor and light fixtures overhead that cast a cold bright hue.

"Here to see Dr. Hargreaves, please," Connor said in a brisk but friendly tone, showing his ID to the receptionist, who was busy juggling two phone calls and what looked like a large pile of admin work on the side.

She nodded. "Autopsy room three. Down the corridor."

Connor handed Cami a mask, which she put on, hoping he didn't notice that her hands were shaking. Then they walked down the corridor to door number three.

The pathologist, Dr. Hargreaves, was waiting for them at the entrance to the room. He was a middle-aged man, with a balding head and glasses perched on his nose above the mask. He wore a lab coat and gloves and had a brisk, professional air.

"Good to see you, Connor. Been a while. At least three weeks since we last discussed results, I guess?"

Cami was sure that in terms of serious crimes, three weeks without seeing a pathologist for a postmortem was noteworthy.

"I was here last week, but speaking to other docs. If I remember, you were taking a few days of vacation? I don't have to ask if you've been busy since you got back," Connor said. "This is Cami Lark, assisting with the case."

Dr. Hargreaves gave her a respectful nod. "Come on in. I'll show you what I found."

Feeling as if she was walking through glue, Cami forced her reluctant feet over the threshold and into the brightly lit room, where the smell of disinfectant and formalin was even sharper.

In the middle of the room, a steel table dominated. A body covered by a sheet lay on it. Cami felt her heart race and her hands shake, but she forced herself to keep her eyes fixed on the table as they approached it. This was what she needed to overcome.

Dr. Hargreaves pulled back the sheet to reveal Kate Minnett's body, and Cami's stomach lurched at the sight of the woman's pale, lifeless face.

She forced herself not to avert her eyes, even though it was the hardest thing she felt she'd ever done. She was going to pay this woman the respect she deserved. She was going to be strong.

But she only managed a few seconds of staring into those cold, blank eyes before nausea roiled inside her and she had to look down, feeling ashamed as she stared at her own sturdy, black Doc Martens.

"What I noticed with both these victims is that their stomachs were empty, and they were also slightly dehydrated before their deaths, as if they'd been without water for a day or so. Furthermore, both their throats were slightly inflamed. I noticed it with our first victim, and this one confirms it."

"I see," Connor said.

Cami stared at him questioningly. He seemed to be reaching a conclusion that she hadn't made yet. What was it?

"They were both held somewhere for a while, and must have screamed for a long time, hoping that someone would hear," Connor explained, and now Cami's stomach lurched violently. A wave of nausea hit her as she took in this reality, causing her to have to breathe deeply as she felt a cold sweat spring out on her forehead.

She was not going to throw up, she told herself. She was not. Disturbing as this was, sickening as the image was, she reminded herself that it had been far, far worse for the women. They hadn't survived. She was here and now needed to catch their killer, and she couldn't do it if she rushed out of the autopsy room when valuable evidence was presented.

"I see," she said in muffled tones, as icy perspiration crawled its way down her temples.

"Not tied up for long—there's faint evidence on the wrists, but I would guess it was just for the journey and then removed," the doctor said.

"Locked away without water. So either a basement, or a soundproofed room, or else somewhere out of town, more remote," Connor was saying thoughtfully, as Cami still reeled from the graphic reality that the throat inflammation was from screaming. Screaming for help while the killer listened and nobody else heard. This was awful!

"No trace evidence, unfortunately, but definitely some signs they tried to escape," the pathologist said.

"Show me?" Connor asked.

Trying to distract herself as the two men then discussed the torn fingernails and bruised hands, evidence of struggling to get out and perhaps struggling with the killer, Cami's gaze fell on the piles of clothing. She stared at them, noting absently how similar they were.

Black jackets, ragged button-down shirts, scuffed blue jeans, heavy shoes.

As her numb mind slowly took this in, Cami's brain finally began to work again. This was odd, it wasn't right. Could it mean something? Was there a clue hiding in this?

Cami took out her phone and quickly checked that she was right. Getting bolder, embracing her theory, she forgot about the sweat now cooling on her face. Instead, she looked more closely, analyzing and comparing the labels, the sizes, and the records of the women in their own online photos.

"If that's all, then we'd better get going," Connor said to the pathologist, and Cami drew a sharp breath.

"Wait a minute," she said to Connor, who glanced around, surprised.

"What is it?"

"There is something strange. Look here, Connor. Can you see it? I'm seeing it." She held out her phone to him, and then indicated the piles of clothes.

"Their clothing?" he asked.

Cami nodded.

"They're both wearing men's clothing. It doesn't look brand new, it's worn and old and shabby. Maybe secondhand, because it seems to be their size, more or less. But I don't see any sign on their social media that either of them dressed that way. Kate seems to have worn skirt suits mostly. And Gracie likes trendy, feminine tops and goes for the color pink. Why were they dressed this way?"

She stared at him and saw his eyes light up.

"That's a very good question," he said. "An excellent question, in fact. You might just have found something important here that could tell us more about this killer."

## CHAPTER EIGHT

Staring at the piles of clothing, Connor felt intrigued and enthused by this lead that Cami had picked up. She was sharp and observant, and something like this, a detail she noticed that deviated from the normal, could be very important.

"So, what do we have here?" he asked. "Can we go through these piles in detail?"

Dr. Hargreaves hurried over to the piles and set out the garments.

"We have normal underwear," Connor saw, noting that in Gracie's pile, the underwear was indeed pink themed. But the rest of the garments weren't.

"You're right," he said, feeling even more convinced that this was significant.

"We have men's clothing," Cami added, pointing to the faded jackets and dark blue jeans. "And shoes, and they are both in their size. But why would both of them be wearing these?" Connor saw her shake her head, and now she was so intrigued by her own theory that some color was returning to her face. "If it was just one of them, I could understand. Sometimes men's clothing is more comfortable than women's. I like men's flannel shirts. But both of them, from top to toe?"

Connor nodded, his mind racing with possible scenarios. "It could be a way of changing their identity. Maybe the killer dressed them in men's clothing to make it harder to identify them—in his mind, anyway, seeing they both had their ID and phone on them when they were dumped. Or else, he wanted the world to know who they were and how he'd changed them."

He was rambling now, he knew, following his line of thinking that might not lead anywhere conclusive, but he saw Cami nodding.

"Or maybe it's something more personal, more specific to the killer's motivations. I wonder if he purchased these clothes from a specific place," he concluded, feeling hopeful.

Connor was now looking at the labels, wondering if there were any clues about where they had been purchased. Cami's guess was right. These items looked secondhand—at any rate, some of them did. They were worn garments, in smaller sizes. Different labels and brands. Cheap clothing. No sign of where they'd been bought. Could be from one of twenty local stores, or online. But these weren't the victims' choices. He had expected the lawyer, in particular, to wear good-quality garments. Her hair, her nails, everything he'd noticed while looking down at her dead body, pointed to her being a lover of quality. Even the gold chain she'd worn around her neck, which had been removed by the pathologist and placed in a tray, was solid and expensive.

So, cheap, old garments. Had the killer bought them and forced the women to wear them? And if so, why men's items? Did this hold a clue to who he was?

It might, but there were no more clues here. The origin of the clothing was still unclear.

"Will you send these in for analysis?" Connor asked the pathologist. "It's a long shot, but there might be a hair, or a stain, or some trace evidence on these garments that can take us further, if they belonged to the killer or were in his possession for a while."

"I'll do that," Dr. Hargreaves agreed.

"I think we can get going now," he said, seeing Cami visibly relax. "Thanks again," he told the pathologist.

He strode out.

As he did so, the suspicion about Cami's activities surged again in his mind.

It had been the result of a tip-off that he'd gotten from a colleague two days ago. The chitchat at the water cooler was that Cami Lark was digging into something that wasn't her business. That she'd been researching things within the FBI—and outside of it—that she shouldn't have been.

Connor was tracing it back to find out who knew. He was disturbed by this. Ethan had been shot when trying to find out—something. Who knew what? And now the word was that Cami was onto something, too.

Connor was concerned for her, and worried about what she might uncover. He didn't know what the hell was going on at the FBI, but he suspected that there was some kind of opposing agenda buried deep. An agenda followed by people who wouldn't hesitate to kill.

He didn't want Cami in danger, but so far, she was stubbornly refusing to tell him what she was doing.

He glanced at her as they got into the car.

Cami was looking straight ahead, her expression blank. Connor didn't know what was going through her mind, but he hoped that she was streetwise enough to know when to back off. Damn it, she was a good kid. Whip-smart and brave, and he'd lost one of his good people just a few weeks ago. He didn't want her to suffer Ethan's fate, but wanted to keep her safe and out of trouble. Even though he'd already seen, multiple times, that she had a nose for trouble and wasn't scared to dive into a potentially problematic situation.

And he was going to confront her about it before this case was over. But not now. This would be the wrong time, because they'd uncovered an important lead, and this was something they needed to take forward.

"So, the clothing," he said. "Why is he forcing these women to wear old, cheap men's clothing? Does it mean something to him? Why would he do that before he killed them? I'm wondering if there's some kind of ritual humiliation involved, maybe a fetish that he has for doing such things, that he's now taking further. And with that in mind, maybe they met beforehand? Maybe he connected with these women and wanted to take things further in that direction and they didn't, or they backed off, and so he tracked them down again?"

"You mean, at a club?" Cami said. She was frowning. He could see she didn't buy his theory that the women might have been part of an underground scene like that, or at least dabbled in it. But one thing that decades of being an investigator had taught him was that people could always surprise you. Always.

Never, ever rule out a theory, however wild, without checking. And that was what they were going to do now.

"At a club or on a website. We have to look at every possibility."

They needed to head back to the police station where they'd been working earlier, where the phones were locked away in that tiny office. Heading there as fast as possible, he drove into the parking lot purposefully.

"Let's hole up here for a while and check out the theories that might fit," he said.

They headed inside. Connor showed his ID and the officer in the lobby gave them the key to their cubicle-sized room. It was quiet at this hour. That was good, Connor knew. Middle of the day, police needed to be out and about. Boots on the ground solved most crimes, in his experience. But right now, good old-fashioned research, possibly combined with some modern hacking, might make better headway in this.

Cami pulled out her laptop and began typing away, delving into the dark corners of the internet that she knew so well. Connor paced the room, his mind racing with possibilities.

"So, how about fetish sites?" he decided.

He moved over to his laptop, picking at the keyboard in a way that he knew amused Cami, or maybe frustrated her. At any rate, she was lightning fast, and before he'd even gotten the words out, her fingers were whirring.

He hadn't even gotten as far as typing the whole word into his search bar before she nodded.

"I've got one here. It's the main specialized site in the Boston area for fetishes, humiliation, BDSM, and so forth. There are a couple of tiny ones that I'm also seeing, but they're more like exclusive private groups."

"What does the main site tell you?" he asked.

"It's got a few hundred subscribers that I can see," Cami told him.

"Search for the two victims. Go back a few months if you need to. If they're on there, even under a fake name, then they were into the scene and we can explore it further. If not, then we look elsewhere, try different sites. Maybe he was into that and they weren't, but there might still be a dating link."

Cami nodded. "I'm guessing they would have used fake names if they were on this site, particularly a lawyer. It seems like everyone uses a fake name here. It's the norm. I'm going to do a specialized location search and also a facial recognition search within the site to see if I can pick anything up. I've got a program on my laptop that can help with that."

Connor waited. He remembered that a couple of months ago he would have felt highly dubious about the process. Now he knew she could do it faster than anyone else, and that if something was there to be found, she'd find it.

But after a few focused minutes, she shook her head. "I'm not finding anything," she said. "I don't see any sign that they were on a site like this. I'll double-check on their phones to be sure."

"Okay. Let's look at the normal dating sites then. Let's go on the assumption that they weren't into this but that he might have gotten into it or be somehow obsessed by it, and that he decided to suggest this to his dates. We must remember that somehow, he found out where both of them lived. So there has to be a connection to be made. Somehow, he got to know who they were, their addresses, and it's significant that they lived alone. Dating sites would be a good source of single people. Generally, at least."

Cami nodded and began to search through the city's various dating sites and apps. It was a tedious process, but he knew that they had to be thorough in their search. He did the same also, knowing he'd be slower, but that he still had to try.

"I'm finding one here that they both used," Cami said. She reached for the two phones. "Kate used it a couple of months ago. Gracie used it earlier this year. I can't see from the site itself whether they matched up with the same person at all, but I think I might be able to do that on their phones." As she started work, she glanced up at Connor again.

Connor felt his focus sharpen. He could see immediately that this was a strong lead, and he held his breath as Cami worked. Let there be someone in common, he pleaded with himself. Let there be someone in common.

After a few moments, Cami let out an excited gasp. "Got it," she said. "I've checked their phones and accessed their messages on this site. They both matched with the same guy. Can you believe it?"

"When?" Connor asked, feeling the same intent surge within him.

"Gracie, about six months ago. And Kate more recently. His name is Gavin Brandon, and he lives in Boston. He's also listed on the fetish side of the dating app, and he used the normal app as well. That was where he matched with both the victims."

A date in common? This was more than he'd hoped for, and he felt a flare of admiration for Cami's skills and speed.

Now, Connor got onto his own database, typing as fast as he could. It was time for him to track down where Gavin lived and worked.

In a focused minute, he had his result.

It was time to go and confront the man who had matched with both the victims, and could have then fulfilled his darkest fantasies by killing them.

# CHAPTER NINE

A match with both the victims was more than Cami had hoped for. Gavin Brandon was a seriously strong suspect. And he lived close by, in a suburb adjacent to Kate's, and not far from where Gracie lived. He would have been close enough to stalk those women.

As they were on their way to Gavin's place, another thought occurred to Cami.

"You said neither of these victims have family who live locally," she said.

Connor nodded. "That's right. Always makes it harder. Kate was a lawyer, worked long hours. I believe Gracie moved away from home a few months ago and came to Boston. Her parents said she was looking to be more independent. I think they were protective of her, if you read the police report." He sighed.

"Do you think that was why he chose them?"

"Because they lived alone?" Connor asked.

"Maybe there were other reasons, but that could be one? Because they lived alone, they were easier to stalk, to take?"

"It's definitely something to keep in mind," he said. "That could be one of the reasons he chose them."

As they drove into the neighborhood where Gavin lived, Cami took a look around, taking it in. This was a hodgepodge area where higher-density apartment blocks coexisted, somewhat incongruously, with straggling small homes. Warehouses on the opposite side of the road presented a looming threat, waiting to consume this dilapidated suburban area.

"Gavin lives in number twelve, but it's the middle of the day. Will he be home?" Cami wondered.

"We'll see," Connor said. "There was no recorded workplace. So if he's not here, we'll have to find out where he is."

"Maybe I can find something on him," she said, getting onto her phone and seeing if his name brought anything up, anywhere, that was relevant.

Engrossed in her research, she barely noticed when Connor stopped the car.

"He does have an online profile," she said. "I'm seeing here that he works in tech," she said, surprised. "He's a programmer and he seems to work from home."

"In tech?" Connor cast her a doubtful glance. "So he could research his victims easily, then?"

Cami nodded.

Gavin being in tech was automatically making her more on the alert. She found herself looking more carefully at his house, searching for hidden cameras or any other signs that he was monitoring his surroundings.

The house was a gracious two-story home with a small yard, which was in surprisingly good repair compared to some of its neighbors. But there were small yet important signs that the owner liked his privacy. Cami didn't see cameras, but she did note the security gate and the burglar bars, and the tinted glass on the front windows, with the blinds closed so that nobody could see in.

Connor pulled up in front of the house, and they both got out, approaching the front door. Connor rang the doorbell, and standing next to him, Cami waited anxiously for a response.

While she was waiting, she wondered what tech opportunities this house might have for a hacker.

His physical security was good, and she could see why. This was a mishmash area, and most likely there were high levels of opportunistic crime. But since he worked from home, had he put as much energy into his online defenses? This wasn't an area where it was likely that anyone would be lurking around and trying to access his Wi-Fi.

It might be worth a try. She opened her phone, taking a look at his Wi-Fi. There it was. She could see it. But could she get in?

If it was highly protected, she knew she might not stand a chance. But if it wasn't, she had a beautifully written program that was able to brute-force non-complex passwords in a very short time.

She set it to run. It might work, but it might not. It depended on factors beyond her control, and that was this programmer's focus on his own online security. Software development and cybersecurity were different areas of specialization. A programmer wouldn't always be paranoid about security, and might have a more casual approach.

Footsteps approached, and she hastily lowered her phone. It hadn't found a way in yet. It had only found a network, and now it was chipping away at the access point.

The door opened, and there stood Gavin Brandon.

He was a tall, slim man with short, curly hair and a guarded expression. Cami picked up a sharp intelligence in his brown eyes, but she didn't see much kindness there. Although that could be because there were cops on his doorstep.

Connor showed his badge. "FBI. We need to ask you some questions."

"Me?" Gavin looked surprised. "What's this about?"

"It's in connection with a case."

"A case?" He stared at them, frowning. At least he wasn't slamming the door in their face. But he still seemed wary.

"Can we come in?" Connor asked.

Gavin hesitated for a moment before nodding and stepping back to let them in. Cami couldn't help but notice the way his eyes flicked over her as she passed him, taking in her appearance with a strangely intimate stare, as if he was analyzing her vulnerabilities, just as if she was a profile on a dating site. She felt a sudden chill, wondering if he knew why they were really there, and had his strategy already in mind.

Inside, the house was neat and tidy, with a minimalist decor that seemed to match Gavin's reserved demeanor. This was not the kind of person who liked to make his home feel like a home. The table in the hall was bare of everything. They entered a sparsely furnished living room, with a large-screen TV and a sleek black couch. Cami took note of the stark, modern furnishings and the large computer setup on the desk. This was definitely a tech person's house.

"What are you here for?" Gavin asked.

"We're here because you're a member on a local dating app," Connor said. "Two women you interacted with have been murdered. We need to know when you last spoke to them, and also a few other pieces of information."

"Murdered?" Gavin's voice was loud and shocked. Falsely so? It didn't seem like real surprise, Cami thought.

"Katie Minnett and Gracie Foster," Connor said. "You remember the names?"

Gavin's face paled slightly as he nodded. "Yes, I remember them. I spoke to them a few times, but I never actually met them in person."

Cami found that hard to believe. Gavin had matched with both women on a dating app, who lived close by to him, and yet he hadn't been interested enough to meet them in person? It didn't make sense. Unless the only reason for connecting with them was that he planned to stalk them.

"When was the last time you spoke to them?" Connor asked.

Gavin paused, clearly thinking. "I never really spoke to them outside of the app. We messaged a few times on the app, and that was it. Katie and I were planning on meeting up, but then she stopped replying to my messages. I assumed she lost interest. I never tried to contact either of them again."

Cami wasn't convinced by what he said. He was fidgeting now, and looking down. She was sure Connor thought his body language was a red flag, but how were they going to prove he was lying?

There didn't seem a way to find that proof. At least, not until she looked down at her phone.

She'd gotten in! Her program had worked. Her theory that programmers were not cybersecurity specialists, and had more casual attitudes, had proved to be correct. She felt a thrill of excitement that her app had managed to bypass the fairly basic security that he had in place. Now, she had a route through to his computer. What could she find there? She didn't see the dating app on his laptop. Would there be anything in his emails?

Unobtrusively, hoping that Connor would keep him talking, she scrolled through the emails, wondering if there was anything to find.

There were reams of work-related emails, so many that she began wondering if this was a total waste of time, because she didn't seem to be getting anywhere. It seemed like all Gavin used his computer for was work.

Although, what was this folder here? This sub-folder? Perhaps this was where he kept his private emails.

Cami clicked on it and went inside.

Immediately, her eyes widened. Gavin was lying. The emails proved it.

Time to drop the bombshell and see what happened.

## CHAPTER TEN

"I never really had anything to do with those two women," Gavin Brandon repeated to Connor, but now Cami felt as if every lying word was hammering the nails deeper into his coffin.

"Actually, you did," she said, deciding to interrupt him there and then.

He swung around and this time, she saw the aggression in his face, visible for the first time, carefully concealed until now.

"What do you mean?" he asked in threatening tones.

"You know, don't you? That you've been sending them messages with explicit content? Invitations and then threats?" she said, feeling a flare of pride, because her software had worked better than she'd thought it would. And faster, too.

"How do you know that?" He made a grab for her phone but she twisted away, and a moment later, somehow, Connor was standing beside Gavin and holding his arm firmly. He'd moved so fast that she hadn't even seen him until he was there. He'd clearly been prepared for Gavin to try to grab the phone.

"I did some research as we spoke," she said cagily. "It's true, isn't it? You were emailing both Katie and Gracie repeatedly. You continued doing that for weeks after they stopped replying. And you were depicting some pretty dark fantasies."

Gavin's face contorted, and Cami could see the fear in his eyes. She had him trapped. He hadn't thought anyone would know about that secret email folder that her digging had produced. Now it was clear that she knew, although she hadn't said how. But the knowledge was enough. Maybe he assumed she'd accessed the victims' emails and got the information from there. She could do that if she needed to. The messages would probably be long deleted, but now that she knew about them, she could track them down, find fragments of them, and piece together enough to provide proof from that side.

"You're lying," he said, but his voice was wobbly as he fell into a chair. "I don't know what you're talking about."

"It seems you were obsessed with both women and that you were fantasizing about hurting them and humiliating them. I think Gracie must have blocked you, and I see here that Kate threatened you with legal action. Then you backed off. But maybe you didn't. Maybe you found another way to get to them."

Gavin's gaze darted back and forth between Connor and Cami, and Cami could see his panic growing with each passing moment. He looked like a cornered animal, and Cami knew that he was capable of doing something drastic if he felt like his back was against the wall.

"Did you back off?" Connor asked sharply.

For a moment, the air seemed to smolder as if it was about to ignite, and Cami tensed. She saw something in Gavin, something disturbing. She worried that he was going to try something violent, that he was going to leap up from that seat opposite Connor and try to strangle him, or that he was going to attack her.

The intent was there. Visible. Tangible. She could see it in the movement of his eyes, the way his legs braced against the floor. And the way that Connor subtly shifted his weight, ready to react instantly to anything this man might do.

And then, with a visible effort, Gavin bunched his fists, digging them into the chair cushion. He shifted his feet on the floor. He took a deep breath. It felt like curls of smoke were wisping into the air.

She knew for sure that this man had a violent side. The emails had proved it. But now, he was exerting self-control.

They had caught Gavin in a lie, but they had also seen a glimpse of his inner demons. Cami wondered how many other women had been on the receiving end of his twisted fantasies.

Gavin stared at Cami, then glanced at Connor, and then he let out a deep sigh.

"Okay, you got me," he said, his voice low. "I took it further than I should have. But I never would have hurt them. It was all just a fantasy. I let my fantasies out that way and I admit I lost control for a while."

Cami wasn't convinced. She had seen the dark depths of his imagination in those emails. She knew he had crossed a line, and the fact that he had kept his violent fantasies hidden away in a secret folder only confirmed it.

Connor leaned forward, his eyes narrowing as he studied Gavin.

"You've been in contact with both victims. And now they're both dead. We need some answers from you about your whereabouts at the time of the crimes. Talk me through your movements last night."

"Last night?" Gavin looked wary.

"From about six p.m. onward," Connor said.

"I was here. At home."

Connor stared at him. "Alone?"

"Alone," Gavin said. Now his jaw was clenching. He looked scared.

"Anyone able to account for your time?"

"I was working," he said. "Look, I know this seems bad for me. You probably think I'm some kind of psycho. I swear I'm not, although I can see how it might look that way. But really—just because I sent a few damned emails?" His voice rose incredulously. But Connor stayed calm.

"Can you account for your time? Were you communicating with anyone?"

Only now did Cami see his tightly bunched fists start to relax.

"I guess I can do that. I had a big project that I was working on all night. For a client in Korea. We were communicating the whole night, testing it out. I've got the message thread, and I've got all the tests we did." He stared at Cami. "If you know IT, you'll be able to follow the track."

"Show me," she said.

"Here. Take a look."

He got up and strode over to the state-of-the-art laptop on the dining room table.

"Wait a minute." Connor held up his hand. "Cami, you look at that record. Mr. Brandon, we're going for a walk."

"Where?" Apprehension was now visible in Gavin's eyes.

"You're going to show me around your house," Connor said. "Come with me. I want to see what's in here, what you've got in your rooms."

In this neighborhood, with its hodgepodge of apartment buildings, warehouses, and dilapidated homes, it might be easy to keep someone imprisoned if you had a soundproof room. This didn't seem like the kind of area where people would hear, or would ask questions if they did. So she guessed Connor was going to check for any hiding places, and in the meantime, she needed to confirm that Gavin really had been programming all night.

She hadn't known what to expect, but as she sat down at the laptop and started going through the message thread, she saw that he wasn't lying. The messages went back and forth for hours, with Gavin sending code and the client responding with feedback. They had run a few tests and fixed a few bugs. It was clear from the thread that Gavin had been working hard on the project from about five p.m. until about two a.m. There hadn't been a window of time where he could have gone out and dumped a body. Not with what she was seeing here. There hadn't been twenty minutes to spare. And she double-checked the IP address that the messages had been sent from.

It was this one. He hadn't gone elsewhere with his laptop, but had in fact been working here.

Footsteps sounded behind her. Connor was returning, with Gavin walking behind him. Connor's face was inscrutable but he gave Cami a quick nod that told her the house was cleared, and he'd found no soundproofed rooms or subterranean hiding places.

"I'm happy with what I see here," Cami said.

"You'd better not have messed up my coding," Gavin said, the threatening note now simmering in his voice again as his confidence returned.

"I didn't touch your coding," Cami retorted. "Why would I do that?"

"We'll leave now," Connor said loudly, seeing that tensions were still running high and a tech-related argument was about to break out. "But I must warn you, Mr. Brandon, you're treading a fine line here. You could have gotten into big trouble from sending those emails. Cross that line again, and things could go badly for you."

Gavin stared at him, clearly not appreciating the advice.

"You've cleared me. I'll live my own life, thank you," he said defiantly, and Connor shrugged.

"Your choice," he said.

As they left, Cami decided that this visit had not been totally fruitless. They might have cleared Gavin, but she thought that he'd given them a window into the killer's thinking. The way Gavin obsessively emailed the women, forcing them to be subjected to his dark, twisted fantasies, yet perceived himself as the innocent party, was a mindset that must be shared by the man they were hunting.

But the hunt was futile so far, and this lead had fizzled out. And worse was to come.

As they left Gavin's house and approached the car, Connor's phone rang.

He picked up, his voice sharp.

"Yes?" he said. "Yes, go on, put me through." He paused, and then he gripped the phone tighter as he spoke the words Cami dreaded.

"Another body? Where?"

# CHAPTER ELEVEN

"You were a challenge! What a challenge you were!"

Breathing hard, the killer forced the woman's limp arm into the shirt sleeve.

"You will wear this, even if I have to make you!"

This last victim, the one he'd taken last night, had surprised him. He'd thought her spirit was broken. She'd been in tears, compliant, submitting to his will. But when he came back to taunt her one last time about the outfit she was wearing, before he came in and killed her, he realized that she'd gotten a whole lot more fighting spirit. In fact, she'd proved to be a wildcat.

She'd stripped off the men's clothing and replaced it with her own, and then she'd refused to put the men's clothing back on. He needed her to! He had to kill the old him, the person he'd used to be.

And he'd gotten angry with her. He'd become impatient, then furious. And then he had stormed into the room where he held her, deciding that he would murder her there and then. He had lost control, a control that he knew he held onto only by a thin thread, as he yelled and screamed and threatened.

He had seen something in her eyes. Defiance, yes. But also a kind of resignation. She had known, as he did, that he was going to kill her regardless of whether or not she followed his twisted rules.

And that had made him pause. For a moment, he had seen himself from her eyes. He had seen the monster he was, the kind of man who killed women and forced their bodies into clothing that didn't belong to them.

It had frightened him. And in that moment of vulnerability, the woman had struck, getting her hands around his throat.

He coughed. His throat was damaged. He was still hoarse from the attack.

He had managed to overpower her, but it had taken all his strength, and of course, he'd had to kill her. His rage, his anxiety, had reached a crescendo and he'd known there was no turning back. And now, as he forced her limp arm into the tattered sleeve of the men's shirt, he couldn't help but feel a sense of grudging respect for her. She had been a worthy adversary, but she had lost in the end.

"What did you think would happen?" he gently mocked her. It was easy to do that now that she was dead, but it had been too soon. Why had he lost control for those crucial moments when she was alive? Why couldn't he have had a better grip on himself?

He deserved his hoarse throat and the scratches on his arms. Long sleeves would cover them. There was a nick on his face as well.

"I had no choice but to kill you. You didn't give me a choice." The anger surged again, but this time, it was woven through with self-pity. He was sorry for himself, he realized. Sorry that he'd been hurt, and sorry that he'd been unable to give this victim as much time as he'd craved. He'd wanted to watch her suffering for longer. She'd robbed him of that pleasure, defied him in the end, but of course, the blame lay with him, too. He couldn't deny it.

"You lost your temper!" Now, as he carefully slipped her foot into one of the scuffed, steel-capped shoes, he realized there was only one person to blame, only one worthy target of his anger, and that was himself. He could get mad at himself and nobody else.

He laced the shoe carefully, checking his watch, feeling worried about the time. It was already getting light, and this was a risk, but he had to take it. He didn't want her body cluttering up his room any longer. He needed to go out and get a new victim and this time, he was going to do it right.

"You always swore you wouldn't be like your mother," he chastised himself. Although he usually kept those memories tightly locked away, he found them surfacing now, as he remembered those horrific punishments. The pain he'd felt at her hands as a child and a young teenager. The humiliation he'd endured. Her broad, impassive face was etched in his mind, framed by brown curly hair, her eyes as bright and evil as those of the devil himself.

All he was doing now was trying to work through his issues. He had promised himself that. Just a few women, maybe four or five of them, to make up for what he had endured, to set the balance right.

He'd grown up in a tough, abusive household. His mother had favored his older sister, and he'd always been the one to receive the brunt of her punishments. He'd been the one who'd been forced to wear cast-off clothing, old garments, who'd gotten bullied at school for his tattered jeans and his shoes with holes in the soles. And of course, he'd suffered his mother's worst punishment and humiliation also, while his older sister had never been touched. He'd been locked away, left for hours without food or water, beaten and taunted.

Sometimes his sister had come past too. He'd known her breathing and heard it.

That door had been locked from the outside at all times when he was in there. His sister had never lifted a finger to open it. She'd never tried to help him.

He remembered fighting the latch, breaking his fingernails trying to get the window open, knowing it was too heavy and stiff and that she would have jammed it from the outside so he couldn't escape. But trying anyway. Trying because he had no other choice and maybe, just maybe, he'd find a way out.

And now he was making his victims do the same, healing himself slowly.

"The only problem is that it's going to be more of a process than I thought," he muttered. "I don't think four or five victims will be enough. My temper is still too bad. I don't have a handle on it yet."

Carefully, he laced up the other shoe.

He stood up and looked at the lifeless body lying in front of him. Her limbs were cool and her face was gray. He felt a pang of regret. He had always been careful not to kill his victims too soon. It was part of the ritual, a dance of power and submission that he relished. But this time, he had lost control.

"Don't do it again! Don't do that!"

It was as if he could hear his mother's sharp admonishing tone in his own words.

He couldn't be on the road to becoming her, could he? Surely not. That would mean that all this had been for nothing. He was trying to get away from who she was, and what she'd done to him. That was exactly why he'd embarked on this process of self-therapy.

It could not be going wrong, it could not! It must be his own fears, messing with his mind.

He shook his head, trying to clear it of the memories that threatened to consume him. He needed to focus on the present, on what he needed to do. He grabbed a large trash bag and began to carefully wrap the woman's body in it, making sure that none of her limbs poked out. She had to be hidden for the journey to the dumpster, which he needed to embark on as fast as possible.

Not many people would be around, especially at this early hour, but even so, any daylight was more of a risk and he would need to be very careful.

Luckily, he'd identified a dumpster that would suit his needs perfectly, in the backyard behind a nightclub on the outskirts of downtown. The club was usually busy until the small hours, and then as quiet as a grave until mid-morning, when the first cleaners emerged to clear the debris of the night before.

"You always threatened to kill me and put me in a dumpster, Mother," he whispered, as he completed the wrapping process.

There. She was neatly trussed in the bags and would be almost invisible in the trunk, under a couple of old blankets that would provide camouflage.

He grabbed a black hooded jacket and shrugged it over his head, pulling the hood up to conceal his face. He checked himself in the mirror, adjusting the hood so that it didn't look too suspicious.

Then, with ease, because he was a strong man, he lifted the woman's body up and carried her outside, placing her carefully in the trunk of his car.

He had done this twice before, but this time it felt different. He couldn't explain why, but he felt like he was crossing a line. As if this was something he needed to keep doing, again and again.

Maybe that was just because the therapy was working, and it was changing him. Just more slowly than he'd expected.

He would find another victim, another challenge. And this time, he promised himself, he wouldn't lose control.

# CHAPTER TWELVE

The knot in Cami's stomach twisted tighter as she and Connor arrived at the scene where the body had been dumped.

It was at the back of a nightclub in a seedy area, a couple of miles outside downtown. She guessed that the place must have been deserted until recently, as the only cars there now were two police cars and the coroner's van.

A couple of onlookers were gathered, staring curiously as the police strung up a wide cordon of crime scene tape.

He must have known about this place. Maybe he'd researched it with this in mind. That was what she thought, as Connor climbed out of the car. She hurried behind him as he strode over to the scene.

"FBI Special Agent Connor here. Thanks for calling me in," he said to the officer who was standing guard inside the tape. "Do we have ID for this victim? Does she have a phone on her?" Connor's voice was sharp.

"Agent Connor, the coroner's just arrived. He can tell you. We realized right away this was a serial crime and we stayed back from the scene," the officer said. "The body was hidden from view. A cleaner who started work at eleven a.m. saw it when he went to the dumpster."

Connor nodded grimly in response. Then he headed toward the scene, detouring to put on foot covers and a head cover. Two forensic officers in white outfits were busy lifting the body out of the dumpster. Cami looked quickly away, but not before she'd seen the jutting leg poking out of the black tarp it had been wrapped in. And the sight she'd expected—an old, scuffed men's shoe on the foot.

The same MO. The same need to dress these women in old, tattered men's clothing.

Oddly, the line that was now playing in Cami's mind was from way back and wasn't anything to do with any crime, and it wasn't anything to do with tech either.

It was her father's voice, harsh and domineering, resounding in her memory.

The situation? Cami had been caught skipping school, and to escape detection, she'd dressed as a boy. It had worked for all of two hours until someone had spotted her and snitched to her mother, and her father had come along, roaring up the street in his police truck, grabbing her from inside the ice cream parlor where she and a friend had been enjoying an illicit soft serve cone.

"Get back home!" he'd raged. "You want to dress like a boy and skip class? How about you wear that getup to school for the rest of the week!"

No wonder she didn't have fond memories of her dad, Cami thought. Even now, when she hadn't seen him for a couple of years, the bullying still made her angry. His need to control, his unwillingness to ever listen, had scarred her.

Connor's voice cut through her thoughts, dragging her back to the harsh reality of the crime scene.

He was staring down at the woman's body, a good few paces closer than she dared to go.

"There was a big struggle here, I think?" he said to the coroner, and Cami's skin prickled with goose bumps at the image this conjured up.

"Yes, it looks as if she has a lot of defensive wounds. I'm hoping we can get some of the killer's DNA from under the nails," he replied. "There are multiple bruises and abrasions," he confirmed, his voice flat and professional.

"Cause of death?" Connor asked.

"Strangulation. Same as the others, I understand?"

Connor nodded, and Cami could see the gears turning in his head.

Cami swallowed hard. She was trying her best to control her imagination, but the image of what had played out was impossible to suppress.

She waited while the forensic officers searched the body, watching as the phone that had been in the purse, dumped in the trash along with its owner, got removed and placed in an evidence bag.

Then Connor turned to her.

"Let's go back to the police station. The phone has to be taken into evidence, fingerprinted, and the processes followed before we can access it. So if we go there with them, we can get to it as soon as possible."

He strode to the car.

"Did she have ID on her?" Cami asked.

"Yes, in her purse, just like the others. Her name's Priscilla Jackson. She's thirty-eight years old. I see her address is a few miles from here. She lives out of town, probably in an area of small farms."

Priscilla Jackson? She was older than the other victims and she hadn't lived anywhere near them. How was he finding them? How exactly was this killer targeting his victims?

Cami felt anxiety flare inside her. Was Priscilla, too, on a dating site? What would happen if they couldn't find a common thread between these women? How many more would go missing and end up struggling for their lives, getting defensive wounds, being dressed in shabby men's clothing before being dumped as if they were trash?

At least they had a phone, and this phone needed to tell her something. As she returned to the car, leaving the officers to comb the scene, Cami felt determined that she was going to get something more this time.

The drive to the police station was silent. Cami sat in the passenger seat, her eyes fixed on the passing scenery, lost in thought. She couldn't shake off the image of Priscilla Jackson's struggle, the defensive wounds, the shabby clothing.

When they arrived at the station, Connor led the way to the evidence room. It was becoming a familiar place to Cami. She sat and waited, opening the other two phones again so that they were ready.

A tap on the door, and the officer brought in Priscilla's phone.

Feeling intent on her job now, knowing Connor's eyes were on her and that every second now counted, Cami plugged it straight into her computer, waiting for what felt like an interminable time for her program to access the phone's security.

This might take hours. Impatience surged inside her and she tried to control it, knowing from experience that yes, devices did seem to have an uncanny sixth sense when it came to this urgency.

She'd always gotten better results at accessing a phone when she had the attitude that she didn't care and had all the time in the world. Now, Cami tried to force herself into that mindset as she stared down at the screen.

"I've got all the time in the world," she murmured, as Connor looked at her, surprised. "All the time in the world."

And then, with a ping, she was in. She'd bypassed the security. Grabbing the device, she set to work, seeing what was open and what had been recently accessed.

"Well, this is interesting," she said, surprised.

"What is?" Connor asked.

"Priscilla had her location tracking turned on and accessed her maps frequently in the past few days. I think she needed to know her way going somewhere." Cami looked up at him, seeing his eyes light up as he realized what this meant.

"So we can track her?" he asked, sounding excited. "Can we see where the kidnapper took her?"

"No, unfortunately. Her phone was turned off at that time. But we can see where she was and trace her route for the few days before that. I'm wondering if the killer might have met her along the way. If we can retrace her steps and compare them to where the other two victims were, then we might be able to tell where it happened."

# CHAPTER THIRTEEN

Had this killer been able to hack into Priscilla's device and get her information during the course of her travels? Cami began working frantically on the phone, trying to piece together the movements that the dead woman had made during the last few days of her life.

With a few different apps open and the emails accessed, the record was telling a story.

"I'm taking a look at her emails, and I'm picking up some information from them," Cami said.

"What are you getting?" Connor asked.

"She lived alone, just like the others," she told Connor. "I think she'd recently gotten divorced, about two months back, and she had started a new job just over a week ago, from what I can figure out here."

"A week ago?" Connor's voice was sharp and eager, and Cami could see why. A week's worth of traveling around town with her maps and GPS activated meant that if the killer had followed her from one of her destinations, they should be able to pick it up.

"What did the job involve?" he asked.

"She was going around to business parks and offices, promoting special offers and subscriptions to a local fashion store. That's what it seems like from her emails and messages. The store sells high-end imported clothing, and this was a way to get more business. I guess it was why she was using the maps so much, because the town was unfamiliar to her."

"I think those locations sound like first prize," Connor said.

"Yes. But there's a wrench in the works here," Cami said, frowning.

"What's that?" Connor asked.

"I'm seeing here that she connected to Wi-Fi via a VPN, and only used her phone's signal when she was out and about. There's literally no history of her using local Wi-Fi. This makes it much harder to hack into her phone and get her information." Cami shook her head.

She could see Connor was frowning. "So in terms of tracking someone, that makes it more difficult?"

This case sure wasn't getting any easier. "Yes. It makes it a lot more difficult and it's not what I was expecting. I was guessing that the three of them might have come across the same person at some stage, somewhere, who'd hacked into their networks and gotten their personal information. At an internet cafe or similar. The other two victims didn't use VPNs and had much weaker security. But now I'm wondering if that's the case at all, because hers is good."

"That means that the killer couldn't have gotten her personal information off her phone?"

"It would have been extremely difficult or impossible."

"Maybe he tracked them in person?" Connor suggested. "A more low-tech solution than we've been thinking of?"

Cami thought Connor sounded enthused by the prospect of low tech, because boots on the ground was where his strength lay.

Cami nodded. "I guess if he saw all the victims somewhere, if he used a hunting ground and followed them, or got information from them in some other way, then he could have done that. I'm just going to check for any other possibilities." She scrolled through the phone. "No dating app. No sign of one, not even deleted. It doesn't look like she was interested in that. And no messages from any love interests that I can see. Just a few work-related texts and texts from her friends in Ohio. She moved out of state when she divorced. Doesn't look like she had many friends here yet."

Connor nodded. "You're getting quite a lot off that phone. Was the divorce acrimonious?"

"Yes, it was acrimonious," Cami said. "Her husband and her split on bad terms. It seems, from what I'm reading here, that he cheated. He stayed in their home, where he's living with the woman he was having an affair with. I guess that's why Priscilla moved out of state."

"Okay. Makes sense."

"Exactly," Cami agreed.

Connor continued, sounding thoughtful, "We need to look at the movements of these three women. Maybe they met someone at a bar or a coffee shop, someone who seemed harmless but was actually gathering information on them."

"A bar? I'm taking a look now," Cami said, scrolling through the phone.

"You finding anything?"

"I'm getting something here," she said. "Priscilla went to a bar twice last week. It's called Endpoint."

"Did the others go there?" Connor asked. "Any common ground between them?"

Cami checked the phones, scrolling through, looking for any check-ins, any signs that the others were there.

"I can't find anything on Kate's phone," she said. "But she didn't use her GPS, or check in to locations, so I can't see where she physically went. She might have gone there with friends, or paid cash, or been there without leaving a trail behind her. There is a message here to a friend, saying that they'd meet at 'the usual' bar, but I don't know which one that would be. I'm looking in Gracie's phone now. If we can get two out of the three, I guess we're getting somewhere?"

"Two out of three would be a start," Connor said.

Cami continued to scroll through Gracie's phone, her eyes scanning for any mention of the Endpoint bar. Any check-ins, any arrivals there, any arranged meetings.

How about payments? Were there any payments she could track? Gracie had used an app for a lot of her payments. In fact, she seemed to use it almost all the time, whereas Cami thought that Priscilla had mostly paid cash.

"Now here is something," she said. "I've got a payment here to Endpoint. It's from about six weeks ago. Do you think that's too old?"

"Six weeks is possible, I guess. And two out of three confirmed as being there is worth following up. Let's go there and see. The barman might remember Kate, there might be camera footage." Connor checked his watch. "It's two p.m. already. So Endpoint should be open. Let's take a drive there, see what kind of place it is, and do some digging."

He stood up, and Cami hustled out of the police station alongside him.

The drive to Endpoint gave Cami the chance to think that this bar was well named. The route led them out of the city, through respectable suburbia, into less respectable suburbia, and finally to a road leading out of town, past a few derelict homes.

There was the bar.

It seemed like a biker bar. There were several motorcycles outside, along with a few muscle cars and trucks. She got the impression, immediately, that this was a rough place.

As they arrived, a customer was leaving, a solid chunk of a man in a black leather jacket with gray jeans encasing his beefy legs. He stared at them, a mistrustful expression materializing on his square, unfriendly face.

He swung his leg over the bike, started up, and roared away.

Connor set his shoulders and jaw in the firm expression Cami knew so well. Then he headed to the bar's wooden door, which was closed.

He opened it.

A swath of smoke hung in the beer-laced air. The place was dimly lit, and the scattering of patrons around the bar counter and at the tables didn't look pleased to see them at all.

The bartender was a middle-aged man with a bushy beard, big-shouldered and heavily tattooed. He looked up as they approached, abandoning his task of wiping a glass with a worn-looking rag.

"We don't serve police in here," he said, glowering at them.

"We're just here to ask a few questions," Connor said calmly. "It's in connection with a serial murder case."

"Well, I don't know anything about that," the barman insisted, his hand tightening around the glass. "And even if I did, I wouldn't share it with the police. We don't trust the cops here. You cause more trouble than you fix. You raid us, you issue fines, you shut us down. I don't need to give you anything. See the sign at the door? Right of admission is reserved, and I'm reserving it now. Go get your information somewhere else."

"I don't think we'll be going anywhere else. Not when what we need is right here," Connor said, but in response, there were a couple of derisive shouts and angry mutters from the patrons nearby.

Cami felt a thrill of nerves that the situation was going to escalate. And fast.

But in the meantime, she had seen what she needed.

Cameras. Above the bar counter and also above the door. This place was well covered. Two cameras, two sets of footage, and if they worked, then without a doubt, she'd know if Kate had also been to this bar.

In this environment, she didn't know if they were going to get easy access to those cameras. Hacking them might be the best option.

As the patrons crowded together and she heard the scrape of chairs as several of them stood, she knew this was going to be a race against time.

# CHAPTER FOURTEEN

"Did you hear me? I'm the owner here and these are my rules. We don't serve police in here! All you do is cause trouble for us!" The threatening words, growled out by the barman, resounded around Endpoint's smoky interior.

Having set her phone to search for the bar's Wi-Fi, Cami glanced nervously at Connor, who was standing his ground. His feet were planted solidly on the floor. His face was impassive.

In this threatening atmosphere, he was keeping icily controlled, while making it very clear that it would be difficult to budge him.

Cami watched as the other patrons in the bar started to shift, their hands inching toward their pockets and waistbands.

"It's not a routine check," Connor insisted. "We're not looking to fine you or close you down. Women have been killed, and we're needing some information. We understand two of the victims, perhaps three, visited your bar recently."

"We're a busy bar. And we don't allow any trouble with people hassling women in here. You think we'd do that? You're wrong!"

"All we need is a look at your camera footage," Connor said persuasively.

"And that's one thing you're not getting," the barman snapped back. "Our footage is private!" The request seemed to have ratcheted his anger even higher.

Cami felt her heart racing. The tension in the room was rising by the second. The patrons were now openly staring at them, all with hostility in their eyes.

"Why not?" Connor asked.

The barman's lips twisted into a sneer. "You think we're just gonna let you waltz in here and take a look at our private property? My customers' privacy is important. You can turn around and walk back out that door, or we'll throw you out."

Why was he being so openly hostile? Cami wondered if he knew something about the murders, or if he was just trying to protect his business. She sensed there was more to it than just protecting his business. He was hiding something.

She needed to try to get into those cameras. If she could take a look, access the footage, or even transfer it to the cloud, then maybe they wouldn't need to stand in this smoky room, pinned by unfriendly gazes, with the background music thumping hard and the sight of hands reaching into jacket pockets, which made her think they were getting ready to rustle out guns or knives.

Quickly, she turned her focus to her phone, trying to sidle behind Connor so that she wouldn't attract attention.

What did she have here?

A Wi-Fi network. That was a good start. That could be the base for what she needed. Could she get in?

With nimble fingers, she opened the hacking app she had used before and started scanning for the network access.

It was surprisingly well protected. She heard Connor's voice as she worked, heard him negotiating with the barman, trying to keep things calm.

He was trying to buy her time. That, she realized. But she didn't know how much she had. And her hacking wasn't working. The code was running, but it was taking too long. She needed more time.

Reminding herself that a calm mindset worked better, Cami tried to keep a cool focus. But it was hard to do when all around her she could hear rising voices, getting closer.

And then someone jostled Connor hard, sending him thudding into her and sending her finger jerking across the screen.

"Last week we got closed down!" the barman shouted.

"It wasn't the FBI. We're not here to close you down. Just to ask questions, and take a look at your footage." Connor was remaining calm, but one calm FBI agent was not going to be enough if these men formed a violent mob, like they looked on the point of doing.

She got back on track. Brought up the screen she was working on. Thank goodness, that sudden movement hadn't deleted what she was doing, but just shoved it to the side.

She'd gotten into the master panel. Here were the cameras. And here was the option to access the stored footage.

Copy it, Cami thought. Copy it while she could, because there was no guarantee in this environment that they were going to get to see it.

She typed out a command to send the stored footage through to an access point in the cloud. It was a little slower than her usual lightning speed because her hands were unsteady.

As she looked up, a mix of frustration and pure terror surged through her. They were now surrounded by a three-quarter circle of angry patrons. Behind them, the barman was holding a beer bottle by the neck.

The barman was picking up his phone, and she thought he was probably going to call for reinforcements. Connor was speaking calmly, telling them to put the bottles down, to go back to their seats, but nobody was listening.

This was dangerous. The men were blocking their way out, so they couldn't even leave. She needed to do something very, very fast, because right now, this circle of men surrounding Connor was becoming way too aggressive.

What could she do? With the footage copying, Cami looked at what else was available to her.

Water sprinklers? That would stop these people. The cold shock of water would deflect what was turning into a potentially violent situation.

She was about to activate those when she hesitated.

Don't do it, she told herself. Bad idea, potentially. She didn't want anything accidentally shorting out the electricity. Not when she needed the connection to the cameras. If the water fried the connection, she might lose what she had now. Time was running even shorter now, but she had to keep looking. There had to be something else.

Then, scrolling frantically all the way to the end of the menu, she saw an option to trigger a fire alarm.

It could be their only chance to get out of there unscathed. She hesitated for a moment, weighing the pros and cons. She couldn't see any real drawbacks, and could only think that this might prove to be an important distraction. Swiftly, she tapped the button

Immediately, the alarm blared, the shrill sound piercing through the dense air.

It was deafening. And disruptive. Immediately, the atmosphere changed. The sense of threat dissipated. The circle wavered, and a few people looked around. One or two strode to the door.

"Get out, guys," the barman shouted. "Get out to the front parking lot while I go see what the hell's going on."

Swearing loudly, the barman put his phone down behind the counter. With a final glare at Connor, he turned and left, opening the back door and slamming it again behind him. Clearly, he was going to find the alarm's controls and disable it. Maybe he'd even check for a fire along the way. At any rate, what she'd done had bought them some time.

Now, reluctantly, the men began to file outside. The fight had gone out of them. With the barman leaving, and the distraction of the alarm, the bar suddenly felt like a different place. Were they embarrassed by their earlier aggression? Cami thought it seemed like it as they shuffled out, and Connor was taking advantage of the situation as they passed.

"This is about serial crimes, gentlemen. Stop and take a look. Do you know this woman? Have you seen this woman in here at all?"

A few of the men glanced at the image of Kate that Connor held up on his iPad. She didn't see any recognition in their faces. One or two shook their heads. At least, in the face of this deafening blast, Connor was making some headway and getting the information he needed.

And then the siren stopped, although Cami's ears were still ringing from the noise. The barman had obviously found the alarm and turned it off. That meant he'd be back here soon, and the patrons would probably filter back in again as well. Cami thought the danger was over. Connor's nerve had held, and her triggering the fire alarm had done the job.

But where was the barman? Why hadn't he come back?

Glancing down to check whether the fire alarm had been reset, which would give her an idea of the barman's whereabouts, Cami stared at her phone in consternation.

This wasn't what she had expected to see at all.

Where there had been a record of the camera footage, scrolling forward as she copied it, there was now nothing. Just blankness, punctuated by the occasional burst of static and wavy lines.

Her heart jumped into her throat as she realized what had happened.

"Connor," she whispered, tugging his arm so that he spun around instantly.

"The barman. He's disconnected the cameras. He doesn't want us to see that footage, and I think he's busy deleting it."

She didn't have time to say more. In a few strides, Connor reached the side of the counter, wrenched open the access door, and powered through the bar area, heading for the door where the barman had gone.

Hoping they weren't too late, Cami raced after him.

# CHAPTER FIFTEEN

Why was the barman erasing this footage? And where was he now?

Questions thronged Cami's mind as Connor burst through the bar's back door and out into a concrete yard.

Behind the bar, across the yard, was a large wooden building that had a couple of beer kegs stacked outside, one or two piled neatly and another few lying on their sides. This was the only place the barman could have gone.

The puddle of water outside the back door, from a leaking gutter, gave them a further clue. Heavy footsteps had trodden through that puddle and then the wet prints led around the back of the wooden building.

"We head that way," Connor said, looking at the footsteps. They rushed around the building.

The back door was partially open. A strong smell of beer came from inside. A few kegs were stored there, together with crates of beer and whiskey bottles. Beyond this storage space was another door, and a light was on inside.

Connor strode through the storage area and into the room, which proved to be a small office.

The barman was inside. He was sitting at a desk, staring intently at a computer screen. As they entered, he jumped up, his face a mask of fear and anger.

"What the hell are you doing here? You can't just barge in like that!" he yelled.

Ignoring his outburst, Connor strode over to the computer and looked at the screen.

"What are you doing?" he asked.

"You're deleting footage, aren't you?" Cami accused, her eyes fixed on the computer screen. There was nothing to be seen there, only the white static and wavy lines.

The barman hesitated for a split second before lunging toward the office's other door, behind the desk, hoping to make a run for it. But Connor was too quick for him. He grabbed the barman's arm and twisted it behind his back, forcing him down onto the desk.

Meanwhile, Cami leaped forward, grabbing the keyboard, her fingers racing, her heart pounding as she wondered whether she would be in time. Was she in time? What was left in the archives?

"What have you got to say for yourself?" Connor demanded as she searched the system. He was keeping the barman pinned to the desk.

"I don't know what you're talking about," the barman spat, struggling to break free.

"You disobeyed a direct request from law enforcement. That's a crime. And you are attempting to delete your security footage after we requested it, and I want to know why."

The barman's eyes widened in realization. He knew he was caught.

"I didn't mean to delete it."

Connor tightened his grip on the barman's arm. "You're obstructing an investigation. That information could help us catch a serial criminal. Now tell us, why were you deleting it?"

"I—I—don't know." He lapsed into sullen silence.

Meanwhile, Cami's fingers were flying over the keyboard. How much footage remained? Had some of it been transferred? She had no idea how long it would have taken. It was a large amount of data, but the program she'd used would have compressed it, allowing it to be sent in the fastest timeframe.

She let out a breath, shaking her head. The footage on the computer here was permanently deleted. He'd set the tape to wipe itself clean, starting from the earliest records to the later ones. There were only a few minutes of footage available, which had been recorded in real time after the wipe, and showed one of the bar's patrons strolling out and heading for his motorcycle.

"It's gone," she said, and saw Connor's jaw tighten. The barman, meanwhile, looked grimly pleased.

"I'm sorry about the footage. I didn't know you needed it," he said.

"Oh yes you did. We told you we needed it as soon as we walked in," Connor threatened.

Had she gotten any in her cloud storage?

She pressed keys on her phone, hoping they had something, anything.

And she was rewarded with a long sequence of data that caused her to sigh in relief as she interpreted it.

"Luckily, I accessed the system and ran a cloud backup a few minutes ago. It got almost everything," she told Connor. "It looks like the only missing data is from yesterday afternoon onward. We don't have those last few hours, but we have everything else. Everything, going back four months, which is the full length of the recording capacity."

The barman stared at her, eyes goggling, looking horrified by this news.

"What?" he said incredulously. "How did you do that? What about privacy issues? How dare you steal my footage!"

"Good work," Connor praised her. "For that, and the alarm. Well done." Then he turned to the barman, speaking in a very different tone.

"We're bringing you in," he said, picking up his phone and calling for backup.

*

The barman, who had been identified as Michael Shores, the owner of Endpoint, looked wretchedly guilty.

Watching from the observation window outside the interview room as she linked her phone to her laptop to retrieve the footage, Cami noted that he couldn't meet Connor's stare. Instead, he was glowering down at the desk where he sat, with his wrists handcuffed to the steel loops. Connor was clearly all out of patience with his sabotage attempts. He had a hard look on his face as he stared at the barman.

They had gone to the closest police station, to save time. The observation room where Cami was stationed had a one-way glass window on the right-hand wall, but on the left, its window looked out over a sports field, with a wooded area beyond.

And in front of her, on the screen, was the footage that could provide them with answers.

While Connor was face to face with Michael Shores, Cami was letting her programs run, feeling thankful that she'd managed to obtain it.

"Tell me why you tried to delete this footage, Mr. Shores!" Connor demanded. Waiting for her programs to run, Cami glanced sideways toward the window, where the barman was shuffling his feet uneasily.

"I didn't think it was important," the barman mumbled, avoiding eye contact.

"You didn't think it was important to comply with a request from law enforcement?" Connor asked incredulously.

"I was just trying to protect myself," the barman muttered, his eyes darting around the room. "I didn't want any trouble."

"What kind of trouble?" Connor pressed.

The barman didn't answer, but his silence spoke volumes.

"You're going to give us answers. I don't care how long we sit here. But you're not leaving until you give us the truth," Connor threatened.

"There's nothing to be found. I'm an innocent man. I'm allowed to make space on my footage recordings. We were going to get new tapes today."

"Then why not give us the old ones, Mr. Shores?"

Again, silence hung heavy in the air as the barman looked away.

Cami could feel the tension in the room, even from behind the glass. But it didn't look as if there would be an easy resolution. The barman's mouth was clamped shut.

The best way of persuading him to talk would be to confront him with evidence that he couldn't deny. And that job lay with her.

Having managed to retrieve most of the footage from both cameras, she had to look through it, compare the two data streams, and identify the faces she needed to see there. She hoped she would find what she suspected—that all three victims had visited this bar and that the guilty barman knew about it, and was either shielding the perpetrator—or he was the killer himself.

# CHAPTER SIXTEEN

It was a race against time. The sooner Cami could get concrete evidence from the footage, the sooner they could pin down this evasive barman, who she was sure was guilty.

Cami had now gotten all the footage available, had collated it, and was using a facial recognition program to speed things up. She'd scanned the available photos of Kate, who was the one whose presence in this bar was still unknown, and also of the other two victims, Priscilla and Gracie, so that she could see exactly when they'd been there.

Now, while Connor was face to face with this evasive barman, she was letting her programs run.

"Why did he delete it?" she muttered to herself, knowing that from the conversation in the interview room next door, Connor was asking exactly the same question while face to face with the obstructive barman.

She was searching for the truth in the records, and hoping to find it there.

There was Gracie! Working from the start of the footage four months ago and fast-forwarding with her facial recognition software activated, Cami saw that the young woman had arrived at the bar with a group of four or five friends. They'd gone in and had stayed for about three hours before the footage had shown the group leaving again, at close to eleven p.m. Looking closely, slowing down the speed, Cami didn't notice anyone else leaving right after.

Gracie hadn't been followed from this bar, and she hadn't come back again. That had been her only visit. Cami could understand why. After having been there once, she hadn't wanted to go back there either.

What about Priscilla?

This footage was more recent. Priscilla had visited this bar just five days ago, and it looked as if she'd stopped by on the way back from work. She was dressed in a smart jacket and carrying a laptop bag. She'd headed into the bar which, Cami saw, surprisingly seemed to be a less dodgy place at night. The diehards seemed to crowd in during the day, she guessed.

Priscilla had been there again two nights later, but again, though Cami watched the footage carefully, she could see no sign of anyone following her out. A man and a woman, holding hands and walking casually, had left a few minutes afterward, and the next person only ten minutes after that.

So, if the killer was using this bar as his hunting ground, he was not following victims out.

But was he hunting there at all?

It all now depended on whether she could find the footage of Kate. The other two had been accurately pinpointed by her facial recognition software, speeding through the camera images.

Cami loved the capabilities of facial recognition software and was hugely admiring of the technology behind it. It all boiled down to math.

As her facial recognition program scanned through the images of the customers leaving the bar, it was reading the geometry of their faces. The distance between the eyes, the distance from forehead to chin, and many other facial proportions. The technology she was using, which was state of the art, identified nearly seventy different measurements.

It was extraordinary to think that a program could turn faces into simple math, and by doing so, pick them out of a crowd with speed and unerring accuracy.

That was what it was doing now. Would it find the third face they needed?

Scrolling back through the footage, searching her hardest, with her program running optimally, Cami wasn't finding what she hoped to. She wasn't finding Kate's face at all, and she'd now gone right back to the start of this recorded footage, four months ago.

Kate hadn't been to this bar in the past four months, and the other two women had not been followed out. And that likely ruled out the barman, or anyone else from this bar, having used it as the hunting ground.

She felt crushed by disappointment. She'd been so hopeful about this. The fact they'd managed to copy it just seconds before it was erased had felt like a massive breakthrough. And now, it appeared, the footage was no use to them, although she was sure there were other reasons why the barman had tried his best to make sure the FBI didn't catch sight of it.

Connor needed to know, urgently, that this was not their suspect.

*"No sign of Kate on the footage,"* she messaged to him.

Then Cami tuned in to the interrogation again. She'd tuned it out while she was hunting for her facial images.

"So, tell me, Mr. Shores, when did you first see this individual entering the bar?" Connor asked.

Cami's eyebrows shot up as she realized that Connor had managed to get a breakthrough. The barman was now sounding more cooperative, and he was talking. In a tight-jawed, apologetic way, but talking all the same."

"About six months ago."

"Did you suspect him at the time?"

"Look, I suspected he was selling drugs, but I had no proof of it. I didn't ever see anything happening."

Drugs? Cami was starting to make sense of where this was going.

Connor leaned in closer to Shores. "Did you see any of the deals taking place?"

The barman hesitated, his eyes darting around the room again. "I can't say for sure," he said finally. "There were a lot of people coming and going. But I did see him talking to a few people on a regular basis."

"Did you ever see him talking to these two women?" Connor turned his phone so that the barman could see.

"No. He sold—he sells—to big groups, mostly. As soon as there's a party atmosphere it's like he knows it and he's in, doing business. And then he doesn't leave till the place closes."

"Okay." Connor checked his messages and she saw his face change. "You're going to need to cooperate with the local police. Allowing a known drug dealer into your bar could get you in a lot of trouble. I understand you didn't want to put yourself at risk, and this guy has a violent history. But if you cooperate, and agree that they can plant an officer there to catch him, you might be able to avoid it."

"I'm sorry I deleted the footage," the barman said. "I thought—I thought I was going to get in trouble."

"Next time you try something like that, you will. And cooperating with police is something you'll need to learn about now. Fast."

Connor scowled at the man before getting up and walking out. Cami rushed to meet him, feeling heavy-hearted by how this had ended.

Shores had been guilty—of knowingly allowing a drug dealer to do business in his bar. He'd clearly dreaded the consequences of being found out by the police. But he wasn't the killer, and this was not the hunting ground they needed.

"You sure about the footage?" Connor asked Cami.

She nodded disconsolately. "Yes. I'm very sure. I feel like I've failed, but there's truly nothing to be found. I saw both the other women coming in and leaving. Nobody else left shortly afterward. Neither of the two were followed. And Kate definitely has not been there in the past four months."

Connor sighed.

"We keep looking then," he said. "There's an office opposite the interview room where we can work. Set up there. I'm going to brief the local police on the drug dealer issue so that they can take over."

"I'll do that," Cami said.

Connor turned away, and then turned back again. Now his face was even grimmer than it had been when confronting the barman.

"When I come back into that office, Cami, I'm warning you. I need answers about Ethan, and what you've been trying to find out. This is important. You'd better have them ready and give them to me. No evasion. And no lies."

For a moment, his gaze pinned her, and she sensed that same feeling of distrust that she'd had when they had first started working together, and had been full of mutual loathing. It was as if the rapport between them, built up over months, had temporarily dissolved, and she was looking at a suspicious stranger.

Cami felt frantic with worry. Connor put the law first, always. If she told him, this would be out in the open. And then what?

Then she was scared to think what might happen.

She headed to the small office, feeling sick inside. In just a few minutes, the time of reckoning would come.

# CHAPTER SEVENTEEN

He was nearly ready. This was his time to do it again, and how he loved to hunt at night. Of the victims he'd taken so far, the ones taken after dark were always the most exciting to him.

He could feel the adrenaline pumping through his veins as he put on his gloves and grabbed his bag of tools. He had carefully selected his victim for tonight, watching her closely for a few days, getting to know her routine. She was beautiful, with long blonde hair and a slim figure.

In preparation for the moment of truth, he'd purchased a sleek gray wig for himself.

This woman worked in the corporate world, so again, mirroring her style had required some research. He had found the perfect jet-black business suit and a pair of shoes so shiny he could see his face in them. A dove-gray shirt and a crimson tie completed the ensemble. He looked ready for a *Forbes* photo shoot, he thought, feeling satisfied. The attention to detail was important to him; it made the hunt all the more satisfying.

The anticipation was making him giddy. It was at moments like this, when the voices of excitement and hope were so strong within him, that he didn't hear his mother's voice at all.

That harsh, mocking diatribe was totally silenced. How strange was it that only when he was standing inside someone else's home, ready to pass his old life on to them, did he feel that he was truly himself?

"You have a neat home," he said, looking around the living room in satisfaction. It had been easy to get inside. Most people's homes were relatively easy. He had some basic experience with disabling alarms, thanks to a short-term job he'd held down a few years ago, working for a security company. It had given him the knowledge he needed.

If an alarm system was too complicated, or security was too tight, or else if he found that his victim didn't live alone, then he abandoned that person.

He had done that a couple of times, because he wasn't stupid, he didn't take risks.

But because time was tight, he'd only been in here once, and he had not been able to purchase any items that were similar to those in her bedroom.

Luckily he'd had a stroke of genius.

This time, he didn't have to duplicate the setup, but could just take what was here! She wouldn't get as far as the bedroom. He would meet her in the hallway when she got home, and it was there that he would pounce. So he could simply use a few of her very own items to decorate her new temporary home in his place.

He went into her bedroom, careful not to disturb anything. He pulled open her dresser drawers, taking out a few of her clothes. He knew he'd have to be extra careful not to damage them, but he felt that seeing them on the bed would create that atmosphere of home that he was seeking.

He tucked them into his bag.

Furnishings?

"I don't think one bedside lamp will be missed, seeing you live alone?" he murmured, bending down and unplugging the lamp that was on the side where she clearly didn't sleep. The other side had a lived-in appearance. The pillow was dented, the bed hadn't been carefully made, the coverlets had just been tugged into place messily.

There was a book lying open on the bedside table and also an asthma inhaler and a water glass.

He picked up the inhaler and examined it, thinking about what he could do with it. Maybe he could place it on the bedside table in the room he'd prepared for her. That would be a nice touch.

He smiled to himself, tucking the inhaler into his pocket. He grabbed the water glass and headed to the kitchen. He filled it up with water and took a sip, feeling refreshed. He felt like he was living a dream—and a very nice one, at that.

"Your home is very comfortable, just like your life. I'm enjoying it," he said aloud. "I'm living your life better than you did. I'm enjoying knowing what it's like to be you. I'm going to make you become me now, and then I'll remove you. Erase you." Oh, why was he mincing his words this way? He might as well blurt out the truth.

"I'll kill you," he said. "But it's nothing personal. Just a process. Stepping into your life will help me to heal from my own. I hope you understand?"

Then he wiped the glass carefully with a dish towel to remove the imprint of his lips and fingers, and set it in the sink.

As he walked back, he caught sight of himself in the hallway mirror and frowned.

He was displeased that scars still remained from the earlier victim's attack. He didn't want to show scars. It was worrying that he had identifying characteristics now which showed he'd been in a fight.

It might be wisest to keep this woman and for him to lie low for a few days, to allow these scars to heal. That would be the safest thing to do.

"It's what I need to do," he decided, slipping his feet into the shiny shoes he'd bought. They were restrictive, and the soles were slippery. They were definitely designed for boardroom warriors, and not for people who might need to get caught up in a struggle. He practiced walking up and down in them. Because, after all, he needed to be able to move in them. When he came face to face with her, if she turned and ran, he had to be able to keep pace and to overpower her. Fast, before she got out of her house. He would have to drag her inside and only then could he change back into his old rubber-soled boots.

"It's what I must do. Be sensible and cautious. Be methodical, and plan every single step of the way," he reminded himself.

But, as he adjusted his tie, he felt a frisson of worry.

The adrenaline was pumping harder now, and he could feel his heart racing in his chest. He was ready for this, and nothing was going to stop him.

What he wanted, what he knew was right, was one thing. But when he lost control, all those good resolutions flew out the window.

He wondered if he would lose it now.

He hoped he wouldn't—with most of his mind, at least.

A tiny, gleeful part of him was begging to let rip, and to unleash his killing rage.

# CHAPTER EIGHTEEN

How long would Connor take? How much time did she have?

Cami felt cold with dread as she waited to hear his footsteps, knowing that he'd still be a few minutes if he had to brief the police.

That gave her time to do something. To call Kieran. Perhaps he'd have some ideas on how to handle this. She needed to tell him that Connor was asking questions she'd have to answer. It might put him in danger, too, and if so, she'd feel that she had at least warned him.

When Cami looked at her phone, she felt a jolt of surprise.

Somewhere in the past few minutes, she'd had an incoming call. With her phone on silent, she hadn't heard it, and it had been one she hadn't expected at all.

Her mother?

She hadn't spoken to her mother for months. Ever since Jenna's disappearance, the conflicted relationship she'd had with her parents had worsened. Her mother had always been the quiet one, worn down and silenced by her father's bullying control. She'd never stood up for Cami the way Cami wished she would.

Jenna had done that, but Jenna was gone.

Cami had left home when she was seventeen, and she'd made her own way. She'd applied for and gotten a scholarship to MIT on her own. She'd taken some odd jobs to pay for what she needed. She hadn't wanted to rely on her parents for a single thing.

And yet now, looking down at this missed call, she felt a rush of emotion.

Should she call her mother back? What could she even say? She couldn't bring herself to talk about Jenna, or to tell her mother about the potential danger she was in now. She didn't want to put that worry on her mother's shoulders. Most probably, her mother wouldn't want to hear she was helping the FBI—even if under enforced terms. Her mother thought police work was dangerous. She'd said so quietly when Cami's dad hadn't been home.

But then again, she might be calling because there had been a problem or an issue at home, because she was ill, or something had happened.

Had she left a message? Cami was pretty sure that if there was a crisis, her mother would have left a message.

But there was no message, neither text nor voice.

Maybe she'd just been holding out an olive branch?

Cami hesitated for a moment, wondering if she should just ignore the call.

Another part of her was afraid of what her mother might say, afraid of the pain and guilt that would come flooding back if they talked about Jenna.

But something within her made her decide to call her mother back. After all, she couldn't keep running away from her past forever. She needed to confront her demons, one way or another. She didn't know what to say to her mother, but at the same time, she couldn't just ignore the call.

Taking a deep breath, she pressed the call button and held the phone to her ear.

But it just rang. It rang through to voicemail. Her mother didn't pick up.

She hadn't left a message for Cami, so Cami didn't leave one for her either. And now, before she could call Kieran, she heard footsteps approach. Agonizing over her mother had meant she'd lost that chance, and in any case, Connor's briefing had gone much quicker than she'd expected.

Taking a deep breath, nerves churning inside her, Cami faced the door.

Connor strode in, pushing it open and then turning to close it behind him. The office where they were now, where she was perched on a chair on the opposite side of the empty desk, felt like a trap.

"So," Connor said. "Cami, I need to know. Tell me. Everything."

She swallowed. She didn't have much to bargain with, but what she had, she was going to try to use. She had to.

"Connor, if I do, I need you to promise me something," she said, her voice thin and wavering, but at least she got the words out; she'd found that courage.

His brows rose. He hadn't expected negotiation and was surprised by it.

"What is this?" he said incredulously. "What do you want me to promise? And why?"

"I want you to promise that you won't tell anyone else."

He was silent for a few moments. “And why should I do that?” he asked, in exactly the same tone he’d used earlier with the barman.

“Because I think there’s something going on within the FBI. I think that Ethan uncovered something and was trying to find out more. I think I’ve maybe stumbled across part of it. Maybe the same thing, maybe not. I don’t know. But I’m assuming it is, because it’s linked to—to someone who left the FBI a while ago. And also to someone close to me.” That was as much as she dared to say.

Connor leaned back in his chair and folded his arms. “That’s a serious accusation, Cami. It’s an extremely serious topic. Corruption, or criminal activity, in the Boston FBI branch? That’s what you’re saying. Are you sure about this?”

Cami nodded resolutely. “I’m sure.”

He sighed. She could see he was looking serious and thoughtful.

“You’re right.” The words shocked her as she waited for him to continue. “If you tell me, I’m responsible for trying to deal with it. And this puts us both in a very difficult situation. If there’s corruption or misdoings within the FBI, I’m not currently aware of it. And I do see why you don’t want to tell me.”

Cami felt astounded. She’d never believed that Connor would be so understanding, that he’d acknowledge the complexity of this situation. She’d dreaded that he would simply force her outright to tell him what was going on.

“I’m so glad you understand. It feels—it feels like a lead weight crushing me. But I don’t want—I don’t want whoever killed Ethan to come after me. I don’t think I’d be able to defend myself. Not even Ethan could, and he was trained and—and had a gun and—you know.” Her voice trailed off. She couldn’t speak about Ethan without turning into a wreck. She knew she wasn’t coherent. Tears were pricking her eyes.

Okay, I’ll make you a deal,” Connor said. “You trust Jacenta, right?”

Her FBI-allocated parole officer? The name brought the sharp, savvy, compassionate agent to mind, with her dark hair and piercing dark eyes. She knew that Jacenta would touch base with her tomorrow now that she was involved in a case. Even when there were no cases, she called and texted Cami regularly.

And she had hinted to Jacenta, recently, that there was trouble. Jacenta was approachable and Cami knew she’d be easy to talk to and wouldn’t judge.

Yes, she did trust Jacenta. And most importantly, Cami didn't think she was involved in anything criminal.

"I trust her," she agreed, clasping her hands tightly, wondering where this strange conversation would lead.

"Jacenta has connections to internal affairs, and that gives her protective privilege in situations like these which I don't have. I would be compelled to take things further. She will not be, and in fact she'll be able to keep the confidentiality and investigate the issue more safely. So, Cami, I need you to tell her what the situation is, and then take her advice on how to take this further. She can give you better advice and she won't be in a situation where she's forced to act, like I would be. Will you do that?"

"Yes." Relief flooded her. She felt as if there was a way forward now, a light at the end of the tunnel. "I promise I will."

"Do it in the next couple of days. As soon as this case is over. Go have coffee with her and discuss it. Cards on the table. Full disclosure. You promise?"

Cami nodded. "I promise."

"Good. Now, let's get back to work," Connor said, standing up and walking toward the door. "We have a case to solve."

Cami followed him out of the room, feeling a lot lighter and more relieved than she had when she'd walked in.

"Where are we going?" she asked. To her, the case had felt stalled. She hadn't seen a way forward. She didn't know if there was one. Had Connor found something?

"I want to take a drive," Connor said. "I want to look at all the routes that Priscilla took in the last few days. The places she went to. The office parks she stopped at. You can get that on the GPS, right?"

"Yes, I can get all the points where she stopped," Cami said, questioningly.

"Sometimes feet on the ground get better results," Connor emphasized. "Points on a map don't always look the same as they do when you get there. And I've got a hunch that there might be something we're missing. If so, I want us both to look out for it."

# CHAPTER NINETEEN

Cami felt eager to know if Connor's hunch was right. Would there be something that they could pick up when those points on a map turned into real-life places?

She was glad to get out of the police station's office, which was starting to feel claustrophobic.

Outside, it was fully dark, and Cami was surprised that the rush hour traffic heading out of town had ebbed, and that there was now a nighttime vibe as they headed into the city. Restaurants and bars were all doing a brisk trade. As they headed to the innermost point of the map, she smelled the delicious aroma of braising meat.

"Food. Everyone needs to eat, right?" Connor asked. There was something about the way he said the words that made her curious.

"I guess so," she said. "Yes. Everyone does."

"Including us." To her surprise, Connor turned off the main road and veered into a drive-through. "What do you want? Soda, burger, fries?"

Cami hesitated, feeling hungry, but also feeling guilty that they were taking time off the case. "I'm not sure," she said.

Her brain was working furiously, trying to figure out what tangent Connor was going off on. She knew he was up to something and she felt very curious about what it was. What, exactly, was he trying to find out on this drive?

"You can't work effectively if you're hungry," Connor pointed out. "So let's eat while we can. Going into the town center to start the journey, then out again and going to all those points, will take fifteen minutes. We might as well eat on the way in, so we can get that done, and then focus on the way out."

"Then I'll have all three please, if that's okay," Cami said, giving in to her now growling stomach.

"Sounds just fine to me," he agreed.

Connor ordered two of the combo deals—burger, fries, and soda. Within a couple of minutes, the car was filled with the same rich smell of food that she'd picked up from outside, and she was hungrily munching.

“Can you use your software to devise us a route that takes in all of Priscilla’s stopping points over the last seven days? Since she started work?” Connor asked between mouthfuls, as they drove into the heart of downtown—which, at this time, was quiet, the office buildings mostly dark, the apartment buildings lit up, and traffic thinning on the roads.

“Yes, I can do that. I can optimize it so that we visit every stopping point in sequence,” she said.

“Let’s get a feel of where she went. Let’s retrace those steps and see if there’s anything that needs relooking at.”

Just as she had instincts regarding IT, she guessed that Connor had similar instincts regarding the practical side of an investigation. But as yet, she wasn’t tuned in to them and had no idea what it could be.

Crumpling up her burger wrapper, Cami got out her phone, quickly collating the routes into one long and rather convoluted zigzag path.

“So, here you go,” she said, activating the GPS to map it out. “This stops at every place Priscilla visited in the past seven days.”

“Good,” Connor said. “Let’s take a look.”

He began driving through the darkened streets, this time not going at his usual impatient speed, but at a slower pace. Cami stared out the window, taking in the places.

A small carpet supply business. A florist’s and a hairdresser. A three-story office park. A small building containing medical practitioners—doctors, dentists, physical therapists. Here was a warehouse that was all closed up and dark.

Cami felt like they were retracing the steps of a ghost, following the trail of someone who had disappeared while leaving only this hint of evidence behind. And in a way, she supposed they were.

They were getting a feel for the places Priscilla had been, the environment she had moved in. It was like they were stepping into her shoes. It made Cami imagine what it had been like for this recently divorced woman, getting back into the working world, and in the tough field of door to door sales. Had she liked her job, had she hated it, was it what she would have chosen or just what she’d found?

They went past the warehouses, through a stretch of suburbia, and then joined a main road that led past more office blocks.

Cami was looking carefully at each place they passed, taking it in, trying to figure out what Connor was looking for, and using all her brain power to try to assess if there was anything strange or irregular here.

A few of the businesses were still operational, with lights on. Many more were closed up and dark.

She reached into the bag, snagging one last fry and munching on it, and it was as she did that, in a sudden wash of understanding, that she thought she knew what Connor was looking for.

She inhaled sharply as she realized, causing Connor to glance at her.

"I think I know," she said. "I think I've figured it out."

"Good," he said approvingly.

Checking the map again, Cami went a step further.

"I even think I might know where it'll be. There are a few likely spots. And one's coming up."

Connor glanced at the map. "Yes. It is. One's coming up now. So let's see if it's the right one."

Cami felt disproportionately pleased with herself for having gotten onto his wavelength and being able to make a logical leap into something that was not tech related.

It was the food that had made the connection in her mind, a connection that Connor had been mindful of earlier.

In a long, weary working day, Priscilla would surely have needed to stop and eat, to sit down, to use the restroom, to spend some time regrouping. And perhaps that was where she'd been noticed by the killer. It made sense for him to use a diner or a restaurant or a coffee shop as a hunting ground.

With that in mind, she watched as they approached the next of the businesses. This was where a few of the dots converged, Cami saw. That meant Priscilla had made a stop here on almost every day that she'd gone out and about. It was a large multi-story office park that looked to contain a number of businesses inside.

There didn't seem to be a coffee shop in the building, but as they drove closer, she saw something even better.

Right next to the office park, on this well-treed street, there was a diner. Brightly lit, attractively advertised, with photos of tasty-looking food in the windows that would have made Cami feel hungry all over again if she hadn't just eaten. There were special offers, co-sponsors, competition drawings with weekly prizes to be won. This diner, named the Zesty Kitchen, was doing a great job of marketing itself to the community.

She stared at it in understanding, taking in the busy atmosphere, the bright lights, the lines of cars parked outside.

"I think Priscilla may have come here," Connor said. "Perhaps this was her stop, not the office park. Or she visited the office park, but also came to the diner. She's been here most days, if I'm right? Most working days, and usually this was her evening stop, at about five-thirty or six p.m.?"

"Yes. Correct," Cami said.

"And people have to eat. We did. So did she. If she came here most evenings, then that might have been where she was spotted."

"And if that's the case, maybe the others did, too?" Now, excitement flared inside Cami, because she saw how this might unfold. It did make sense that Priscilla would have stopped somewhere to eat. And a woman on her own, stopping in a diner in the evening, was likely to live alone. It would have made it easy for the killer to choose her.

"If this is his hunting ground, we need to confirm it first. Now we know where it is. We know she went there most evenings, once or twice at lunchtime. She was a regular there, for sure. But there might be other places along the way. So before we focus on this, we're going to finish the route and check for any other stops where all the women might have ended up," Connor said.

Cami felt as if the case had restarted again and was speeding forward.

With all the victims' phones, and all these points on the map to explore, she felt sure they could piece together the puzzle. And this time, it would lead them to the killer.

# CHAPTER TWENTY

Back at the police station, Cami got to work. She had a target location—the Zesty Kitchen.

Now all that was left was to connect the dots and see if the other victims had been there. If so, then they had pinpointed the killer's hunting ground.

There had been no other possible places along the way. She and Connor had checked carefully, driving to every single location on the map route, not wanting to leave out a potential destination by being too complacent or stopping the search too soon. That diner was the only place offering food where Priscilla had routinely stopped, and Cami felt hopeful that it was the key to this.

She sat down at the desk in the tiny office and pulled out her laptop. She began to search through the GPS data on the victims' phones, checking for any evidence that they had also visited the diner.

GPS wasn't the only way she could track their movements, and in any case, Kate's phone didn't have it activated at all. So she'd have to look for other ways.

Payments. That was top of mind. A payment to the diner would be the proof she needed.

Cami quickly accessed the bank transactions of the victims and began to scan through them, looking for any credit card transactions that were made at the diner.

Immediately, she saw one on Priscilla's phone. She'd paid for her dinner every day, so Connor was right. She had chosen that place as her regular eating spot.

What about Gracie? Cami turned to the second phone, accessing all the possible apps she used for payment, and checking carefully through her texts as well, in case the bank had automatically texted her when a payment went through.

There! Not a credit card transaction, but there was something on Gracie's payment app. She'd had dinner there about two weeks ago. The amount was enough to cover a meal for one, and Cami guessed that's what she'd had.

So, what about Kate? Was there anything she could find?

Cami's heart skipped a beat as she scrolled through Kate's bank transactions. What was this?

There was a credit card transaction from three weeks ago. And yes, it was for the Zesty Kitchen. She must have stopped there late in the evening, probably after a work function or meeting, Cami guessed. At the same diner. Without a doubt, all three victims had been there.

"I've got it," she said to Connor. "They were all there."

"Good work," Connor said. "It's time to get on-site now. This must be the place. And now, we need to find the person."

*

Cami couldn't believe that after so many false starts, so many wrong turns, they were finally on the right track. What would they find at this diner, which all three women had visited in the past three weeks?

As Connor pulled up outside, she stared at the brightly lit facade. From the outside, she could see the tables, the patrons reading menus, the smiling waitresses bringing drinks. It seemed like a homely place, a comfortable and safe spot for anyone to have a meal. She could see why women on their own had felt at ease coming here at night.

"I'm going straight to the manager," Connor said. "First thing, we need to take a look at the staff. They would have been the best placed to see who came and went here. Also, we need to remember the last victim, Priscilla, fought back. So, staff members with visible injuries, anyone who's got cuts or scrapes, any unscheduled absences, are suspicious."

"And then the restaurant patrons?" Cami asked. Connor nodded.

"Then we look at the regular clientele. Who's been around at the same time as the victims. Cameras will help us."

Cami thought this was a solid plan. It seemed to cover all bases.

They entered the Zesty Kitchen and were greeted by the warm, inviting atmosphere. The smell of grilled meat filled the air. Copies of edgy modern art paintings lined the walls, giving the place a memorable character. Music from the eighties and nineties wafted from the loudspeakers.

Connor headed straight for the counter.

"Table for two?" the receptionist greeted them with a cheerful smile and a tilt of her curly blond head.

"No, thanks." Connor showed his badge. "FBI here. We'd like a word with the manager. We need some information."

"FBI?" She paled. "Is—is this place in trouble?"

"We're seeking information at this stage. That's all."

His words weren't exactly reassuring, and the receptionist looked even more disturbed as she turned away and hurried to a closed door. Tapping on it, she waited, calling, "Mr. Gaynor? It's urgent."

Cami looked around, checking what surveillance they had here. There were cameras, but they pointed toward the till, and were clearly designed to discourage staff from taking money, rather than to keep track of customers. There might be others outside, she guessed. Perhaps there were cameras in that big parking lot beyond the diner.

The office door opened, and a genial-looking, gray-haired man hurried out.

"Sorry, Carly, I was busy on a call," he said. "What's the problem?"

Turning to the reception desk, he saw the FBI badge Connor was holding out, and the same startled expression crossed his face.

"We need some information from you," Connor said. "You're the manager here?"

"I am the owner. Tom Gaynor. I have no idea what this is about, but could we talk in the back?" He glanced around the diner as if worried the customers might be affected by this police presence.

"We can do that."

Tom opened the office door and raised the hinged portion of the counter for them to walk inside. Cami and Connor walked behind the reception area and into the small office beyond. There was only one seat at the desk, so they all stood.

"We're investigating serial crimes," Connor said, as Gaynor closed the door. "Three women have been murdered, and all of them were at your diner in the past few weeks."

He looked flabbergasted, his blue eyes opening wide.

"My diner?"

"Correct," Connor said.

"And you think one of my staff might have had something to do with this?"

"They would have interacted with the customers? Had access to the payment information, the customer info?"

He looked pale. "We don't keep that a secret. I mean, anyone can see it, yes."

"Any of your staff?"

"The front of house staff, yes. Not our dishwashers or cleaners, no."

"Have you been at this business the past few nights?" Connor was obviously looking to clear the owner straight off.

He nodded. "I work six days a week, on-site, from eleven a.m. to midnight. Long hours, but that's what it takes. Mondays are my only day off, and that's when our assistant manager takes over."

Kate had disappeared on a Wednesday evening. So the manager was cleared, Cami guessed, watching as Connor jotted down some notes. The most recent victim, Priscilla, could have been dumped early in the day today, and it was still uncertain when she'd been taken. The diner wasn't open in the mornings, so Wednesday evening was the best time to rule out the suspects.

"Which of your staff were off on Wednesday afternoon, into the evening? Either scheduled or unscheduled absences, please," Connor said.

Gaynor frowned.

"We had three of our front of house staff off on Wednesday late shift, which runs from two p.m. until we close after eleven. Dale Churm, Bobby Howes, and Cody McGovern. Other than that, everyone was here. No unscheduled absences. Cody's our assistant manager."

"I'd like to speak to all of them, please."

Mr. Gaynor was looking stressed. "We're very busy tonight," he pleaded.

Connor shook his head. "There's going to be no easy way to do this. We need to speak to all of them. The sooner you can get them here, the sooner we can finish up with them." He paused. "And we're also going to need access to your computer and camera footage, most likely."

"All that?" Gaynor looked horrified. "I don't know if I can allow you access. I've got confidential information stored there."

Connor remained firm. Cami guessed he was going to come across hardcore and not even give Gaynor the option of refusing. And so he did.

"Two choices. The easy way or the hard way. Either you cooperate as a local business looking to assist the police, or else we'll get a warrant and bring in a team and close you down for the night." He paused. "Maybe two nights. We have more than enough evidence, with all three victims having been here."

Gaynor was now looking nauseous with worry. "No, no, I'm not obstructing you. Not even intending to do that," he gabbled. "I was just—just running through things in my head. It’s better that you work here now, and of course I’ll cooperate fully.”

“Let’s start with the first staff member then, if you could call him in?”

“Sure,” Gaynor said. He hurried out.

One by one, Cami hoped, these three staff members would either be cleared, or else they would have a strong suspect.

First in was a tall, blond man of about thirty years old. He looked nervous to be secluded with the police, but Cami thought he had a helpful and open expression. He twisted his fingers together as he faced them.

“Good evening, sir and ma’am. I’m Bobby Howes,” he said.

Connor looked him over carefully. Cami could see no cuts or scratches on his face or his arms, and they would have been visible as he was wearing the restaurant’s branded red T-shirt.

“Just need to ask you some questions, Bobby. First up, where were you on Wednesday?” Connor asked.

“Wednesdays, I go to night school,” he said. “I’m studying business management part time. My class runs from five p.m. to nine p.m.”

“And where do you stay?”

“I stay in a rental apartment with three friends. One of them, my girlfriend, attends the same class. We drove there and back together.”

“Okay,” Connor said. “I need proof of that, please.”

Cami moved over to check the man’s phone and confirm his whereabouts. She did it carefully, not wanting to miss an important detail. But the evidence added up. She looked at the class timetable, the notes he’d taken, and the messages he’d sent afterward saying they were driving back via a pizza place, and did anyone else want anything. He’d even made a payment that confirmed where he’d been.

“I’m happy with that,” she said, handing back the phone to a very relieved-looking Bobby Howes.

The next waiter was Dale Churm.

“You’ve got a nick on your chin,” Connor said, as he walked in, and Cami’s head jerked up in surprise. Could this be the sign of the fight they were looking out for?

Dale Churm, a tall, lanky man with a straggly goatee, was staring in concern at Connor. Sure enough, there was a nick on the side of his face.

“I did it shaving my beard!” He sounded worried. “I’ve been trying to get it into shape.”

"Your movements Wednesday?"

"I went to an ice skating show with friends. That's why I was off work. The show was from six to eight in the evening. We had drinks before, and dinner afterward. I can show you the tickets? And the photos?"

Anxiously, he scrolled through his phone, showing Connor the proof of his whereabouts. Connor nodded, and Cami could see he was satisfied. This was not their suspect. He left, and then they waited.

"We're going to need to see which staff accessed the customer info and what details were available," Connor muttered.

"Yes, I want to know about the regular customers also," Cami said. "I think that's going to be important. Who came into this restaurant at the same time these three women were there? And who left at the same time, and could have followed them?"

"We can do all that, but in the meantime, where's the third staff member?" Connor consulted his list. "Where's Cody McGovern?"

He walked out of the office, on a mission to find out.

"Mr. Gaynor?" he called to the owner, who was now bustling around the grill, supervising orders. "We still need to speak to Cody McGovern."

Gaynor checked his watch, looking surprised.

"He was supposed to be in today," he said. "He was supposed to be in at six p.m. but I see he's not here."

The receptionist glanced around. "Cody called earlier. He said his girlfriend was sick and he had to stay home to help her. Shall I call him and tell him the police need to speak to him?"

Cami and Connor exchanged a glance, and she knew, with a flash of excitement, that this could well be their suspect.

"No." Connor shook his head, and Cami could hear the thinly veiled urgency in his voice. "Don't call him. But please give me his home address. We'll take a drive and speak to him there."

# CHAPTER TWENTY ONE

Connor felt the pressure bearing down as he sped to Cody McGovern's house.

Night was here. This was when the killer would pounce. And he knew they were lagging behind. The next hour would be a critical time.

Back in the diner, he'd had to make some tough decisions, knowing there was a strong chance that the killer was Cody McGovern, and that he needed to get face to face with him as soon as possible, and before he could be warned.

But at the same time, there were urgent jobs to do at the diner. The access to the customer information needed to be checked and also, the regular customers who'd been there at the time the victims were there needed to be identified.

He had to triage the situation in a way that would allow them to be most effective. After putting together the best course of action in his mind, he'd shared his plans with Cami.

"I'm going to say, at this point, we split up," Connor had told her. "I'm going to have to check Cody out and see if this story is true. But since we also need to check the customer records and look at the regular clients, I think you should stay and do that, because it's your area of expertise. You happy with it?"

He knew he would be the one going into the bigger danger. If Cami stayed in the back office to do the checking, he thought it was acceptable for her to work on her own.

Cami had nodded, her expression determined.

"I'll get started right away," she'd said.

He remembered the way she'd warned him as he left.

"Be careful," she'd emphasized.

"You, too," he'd replied.

They were dealing with someone deadly and unpredictable and, as yet, this person was unknown to them. This had to change. Two victims had been bad enough. But three?

Shaking his head, trying to rid himself of the voice inside telling him he'd failed, he went over everything they knew about the case so far as he drove.

Three women, who'd all been customers at the Zesty Kitchen, and who all lived alone. There had been subtle signs of forced entry, though no forensic evidence, so the killer must have sneakily found a way in and disabled alarms if he needed to.

Unfortunately, Connor knew, finding a way in was all too possible. People were innocent. Very few locked their homes up like Fort Knox if they considered their neighborhood to be safe. There usually was a way in to be found, through a convenient window or forcing the back door.

Maybe he ruled out those with very tight security. Putting himself in the killer's shoes, Connor guessed that was what he would have done. He would have scouted out their homes and decided whether it was possible to access them.

As he drove, he wondered what kind of person Cody McGovern was. Was he the killer? What kind of motive could he have for these crimes?

He hoped that if it was Cody, he'd be able to confront him and arrest him quickly.

At that moment, his phone rang.

It was his boss, Fraser, on the line, and Connor knew that Fraser would be demanding answers. Checking the GPS and moving into the fast lane, he took the call.

"Connor, what's the status on the case?" Fraser's voice was urgent.

"We've identified a diner where all the victims visited recently, and I'm on my way to speak with a possible suspect, Cody McGovern, who works there. We've cleared all the other staff so far," Connor said, trying to keep his tone calm. "Cami is going through the customer records and trying to find any connections or leads on that side."

"Good, good," Fraser said. "Listen, we need to wrap this up quickly. With the third victim, we can't contain it any longer. The press is all over this story, and the higher-ups are getting pressure from the mayor's office. We need a suspect and we need a conviction ASAP."

Connor gritted his teeth. He knew the urgency of the situation, but he also knew that rushing things could lead to mistakes.

"We're working as fast as we can, and I'll update you," he said.

"Please," Fraser said, before hanging up.

It was strange that now, when he spoke to his boss, Connor felt a flicker of doubt.

He was sure he could trust Fraser. Wasn't he?

But from what Cami implied, Ethan had been shot after looking into something within the FBI that overlapped with something Cami had been digging into as well.

That changed things, and the knowledge weighed heavy on Connor's mind.

He couldn't let that distract him now, though. Cody McGovern was his priority, and he needed to find out if he was the killer or not.

Cody lived out of town, which already had Connor on the alert, as a quieter, bigger place would create more opportunity for a captive woman to be held.

And there, ahead, down a long, winding driveway, was the house itself.

Connor parked his car at the end of the driveway, trying not to make too much noise as he stepped out and made his way toward the house. There were a couple of other cars parked further down the street. The driveway was lined with trees and the house was tucked away, hidden in a dense outcrop of woods.

Connor walked slowly up to the garden gate. He was watching and listening hard. There were no lights on in the windows—that he could see, anyway. But something was prickling his instincts.

It was the front door. Approaching it, he saw that it was open—just a crack, but enough for him to be sure that somebody must be at home.

At home, in this darkened house, with the front door partially open?

Something was very wrong here.

Connor pushed the door wider, his hand reaching for his gun, touching the grip, making sure it was ready if he needed it. He wasn't a man to shoot unnecessarily, but he knew he also needed to be very careful he wasn't walking into a trap.

The house was steeped in gloom. Only a small lantern on the wall provided a flickering point of light. He stood for a while in the hall, letting his eyes adapt to the dim glow. He had a flashlight, but didn't want to use it yet. Not until he'd allowed himself to see and hear if there was anything inside.

He slowly walked toward the living room, his footsteps silent as he tried to keep his breathing steady.

Dark shapes of furniture loomed. The faint light filtering through the window was from the moon, peeking from behind a veil of cloud. Where was everyone? Again, he had the cold premonition that he was walking into a trap.

Then, turning away from the living room and heading toward the kitchen, he saw another door in the corridor. This one was also ajar.

And it opened onto a steep flight of stairs.

This house had a basement or a cellar—an underground room that he hadn't guessed was there, and that he was only seeing now.

And, as he listened, Connor heard a faint but persistent bass-note thumping coming from that direction.

Shivers prickled his spine. Now it was time for the flashlight.

He turned it on, illuminating the steep, concrete staircase that led down this dark tunnel. Faintly he could see the solid wooden door at the bottom.

Taking a deep breath, he walked down the stairs, slowly and silently.

He got to the bottom. Standing outside the door, he could hear the thumping was louder.

Time to open it. Now, speed and surprise would be his friends.

Connor took a deep breath, counted to three. He didn't know if the door would be open or closed, but he was going to gamble that it might be unlocked.

On the count of three, he twisted the handle hard and shoved his shoulder against the door.

With a crash and a scream of hinges, he burst into the underground cellar.

# CHAPTER TWENTY TWO

Cami's fingers flew over the keyboard, the clicking of the keys filling the small office as she began her search.

Staff access to the system, and regular clients who'd been at the diner at the same time as the victims. Those two priorities were what she was hoping to narrow down, as she holed herself up in Tom Gaynor's office and searched through his computer system.

She'd done a quick check on the camera footage. As well as the camera facing the till, there had been one in the customer parking lot that recorded the license plates of the cars leaving, and there had also been one behind the restaurant, focusing on the staff parking lot and the trash cans.

As she scrolled through the files on the computer, Cami noticed something strange, squirreled away inside a sub-file. It was a folder labeled "Private," with a password required to access it. Something about the folder made her feel uneasy, like it was a secret that was intentionally being kept hidden.

Suddenly, a knock at the office door made Cami jump. She quickly minimized the screen and turned to face the door.

It was Tom Gaynor. The diner's owner had brought Cami a soda and a coffee. His expression was a blend of anxiety and the desire to help.

"All going okay? I thought you might like some refreshments," he said with a nervous smile.

"Thanks," she said gratefully. That was very thoughtful of him. Unless, of course, coming in with drinks was just a way of checking up on what she was doing. That was a possibility she couldn't ignore.

"Is there anything you need?" he inquired. "Anything unclear, anything I can explain to you? Are you able to access the cameras?"

Cami weighed up the pros and cons of asking him about that folder. It might be better not to. She didn't know if it was relevant, and didn't know if she was even allowed to go into it. It had been well hidden and perhaps he hadn't thought she'd find it. If he refused when she asked, it would put her in a difficult situation. If he got mad at her for asking and threw her out of the office, she didn't have Connor with her to use his authority and FBI status to get what was needed.

So for now, it would be better to say nothing.

"I'm fine for the time being," she said. "I'll let you know if I need anything."

"Good," he said, giving a worried glance at his computer. Cami knew that not even an innocent person would let a third party search through their work files without some level of concern. She was sure he was regretting his offer, but figured that he wasn't a man who broke his promises.

Now to hack the password that would allow her access to "Private" and see what was inside.

She set the software to run, and in the meantime, took a look at the payment details that were saved on the system.

The credit card numbers were automatically recorded when a client paid that way, but how much information would those actually give?

The addresses of clients were not visible on the card payment slips. No addresses appeared with the payment details.

"Okay," she muttered to herself, taking a swallow of coffee as she thought about that. "So none of the staff could have accessed the details of customers. It's looking more and more like it was a customer who waited in the diner and physically followed them out. Now I've got to find out which customer."

Even the cash payments, she saw, were recorded with the table number and the name of the person who'd ordered. She'd seen already that this diner was a real family business, a place where people were greeted on a first-name basis. It made her sad to think that such a place could have been misused, that trust abused, with a deadly result.

Cami was a student who had her favorite places around town, and she knew the sense of trust was an important factor, and one she looked for. She wanted to feel safe when she went out on her own and after dark. That someone had abused it here was unacceptable.

So, the first step was to figure out when Kate, Priscilla, and Gracie had been here, and then look at the other customers of the restaurant, and if the same person had been waiting there when all three women had walked in.

She was now sure this was what had happened.

Cami continued to scroll through the payment details, taking note of the dates and times of when the three victims had been at the diner.

She felt a sense of responsibility, as if she was not only solving a case but also bringing justice to the victims. It was too late for them, but if she could find this killer, at least it would mean that nobody else suffered this same terrifying and violent end to their lives.

Kate had been here on a busy night. Almost every single table had been occupied. So it was going to be important to collate the information carefully. If the killer had been part of a group, then his name might not have been recorded—but being part of a group wasn't so likely. She thought he'd have been there on his own, so that he'd been able to get up and follow them out immediately.

So, tables of one person on their own was where she should focus, Cami deduced. There had been five of those when Kate was here.

She made a note of their names. Two had paid cash. Three had paid by card.

Now, Gracie. She'd been here twice. Once at lunchtime and once in the evening. Were any of the same people there?

Not at lunchtime. There was no overlap there at all. But in the evening, Cami saw, there had been. Two of the same customers. Toni Gregor, who'd paid cash, and Zack Overton, who'd paid by card. They'd both been there on the same night as Gracie, and also when Kate had been there.

Now to find out if Priscilla, who'd eaten at this diner three evenings since starting her new job, had any of those customers in common.

Cami took a look, searching through the bookings, feeling her heart pounding in anticipation as she waited for a result.

Then she drew in a deep, quick breath.

There was one!

Zack Overton had been at this diner when every single one of the three victims had been there. On Tuesday night, he and Priscilla had been at the diner at the same time. That made it a hat trick. They had answers now, and those were staring her in the face.

She narrowed her eyes, her mind racing, already reaching for the phone to let Connor know.

And then she jumped as the office door banged open and the owner rushed in.

"Sorry, sorry," Gaynor said hurriedly. "Did I startle you? I'm just getting the spare credit card machine. Have you found anything so far?"

Cami nodded. Now that they were so close, it couldn't hurt to ask, could it?

"Your customer Zack Overton," she said. "He was here at the diner at the same time as every single victim."

She'd expected shock, horror, or maybe irate defensiveness from Gaynor. But she hadn't expected him to look sad.

"I know, it's such a tragedy," he said.

Cami stared at him, feeling as if her reality had shifted.

"I'm sorry, did you say a tragedy? What tragedy?" she asked.

Gaynor sighed. "Zack was seriously injured in a motor vehicle crash on Wednesday morning. He's in the hospital with a punctured lung and several broken bones. I feel so bad for him, because he's such a good guy. I went to visit him yesterday on the way to work, and he's in so much pain."

Cami felt as if she was on a rollercoaster ride here.

Zack, the only customer to have been at the Zesty Kitchen when all the victims were taken, the prime suspect, couldn't have done it.

Her solution had been ripped away just as she'd been thinking they had found the killer.

Gaynor headed out of the office with the card machine and Cami sat, feeling bludgeoned by that backlash of fate.

She didn't have a suspect at all. She had a big, fat dead end with nowhere left to go.

And then a ping from the computer distracted her. In the hunt through the customer records, she'd all but forgotten about that password protected folder marked "Private." Now, her software had cracked the code.

She could access this folder, and whatever was in here, it was her very last chance.

Hoping that the folder held answers, and that there was a reason why it was so carefully hidden away, Cami clicked on it.

A moment later, it flashed open, and she stared at the screen in astonishment.

She couldn't believe what was here.

Names. And not just names, but addresses with them.

# CHAPTER TWENTY THREE

Connor barged his way into the underground room, one hand on the door, the other holding his flashlight. He was ready to grab his gun, but needed to see what was there before he could shoot.

Then he stopped in his tracks, gasping in a surprised breath. He felt astounded by what was pinned in its beam.

The thumping music was blaring from an old-fashioned radio set up on the wooden table in the center of this darkened room. And at the table, five men and two women sat, wearing formal jackets and evening gowns and fancy hats on their heads. The cards displayed on the table, and the piles of casino chips, told Connor that a game of poker was underway. The air smelled of beer and bourbon.

His arrival caused consternation.

The dark-haired man in the chair closest to him jumped up in a panic, knocking over his whiskey glass, his bowler hat falling off his head. The woman next to him, in a purple velvet jacket, grabbed the glass, shuffling the cards and chips out of the way of the spill. There were cries of surprise and alarm.

"FBI. What is going on here?" Connor demanded, his voice booming in the small space.

"I thought you said we were allowed to play poker for money! Why are we getting raided?" the blond woman at the far side of the table said in accusing tones, staring at the dark-haired man closest to Connor.

That man had gone very pale.

"Of course we're allowed to play poker!" he said shakily. "I don't know what this is about."

"Are you Cody McGovern?" Connor questioned.

"Yes, I am. That's me."

"You called in off from work. Said your girlfriend was sick."

"They send the FBI out to check on that these days?" another man, with a wry, humorous face, wisecracked from the opposite side of the darkened table. There was a snort of laughter from the man next to him, but everyone else looked highly stressed by Connor's untimely arrival.

Cody shifted his feet.

"It's—it's actually my girlfriend's birthday," he admitted. "And we decided to have a small party, speakeasy theme, and play some poker. I know I should have been truthful with work, but they can get difficult about personal time off. So I'm afraid I did lie to them."

Connor could see the guilt in Cody's eyes, but he didn't know if it was just from being caught out or for a bigger reason. He scanned the rest of the group, noticing that some were still nervously holding the cards and keeping their eyes down, while others were staring at him with a mix of fear and defiance.

Taking in the decor of the room, it did look like a speakeasy, with liquor bottles lining the shelves and dim lighting casting shadows across the faces of the players.

"I need to speak to you outside," he told Cody. "The rest of you can carry on."

He wasn't going to shut their party down, even though he knew he'd dampened the vibe. All he needed was an alibi from this one man, who was now following him to the door, looking stricken, as if his evening had turned into a nightmare.

Connor led the way up the steep stairs and into the darkened living room, where he turned on a standard lamp. In its glow, he could take a better look at Cody.

He had a couple of scars on his face, Connor saw, but they didn't look recent. Even so, it was worth asking about.

"Your face. What happened to it?"

Cody flinched at the question, before answering. "It was from gravel and broken glass. I was in a bicycle accident a few months back."

Connor nodded, accepting that explanation.

"And your movements on Wednesday? You weren't working at the Zesty Kitchen on that day. Tell me what you did."

"Wednesday? I was here at home."

"Alone?"

"My girlfriend, Tracy, was also here," he said. "She was sitting next to me downstairs. She can confirm that."

Connor scrutinized Cody's face, waiting for any signs of deception or guilt. But Cody was looking back at him with honest confusion, as if he truly didn't understand what was going on.

"Is there anything else you want to tell me about Wednesday, Cody?" he asked, his voice level and calm.

Cody hesitated, nervously running his fingers through his hair. "No, nothing else. It was just a regular day off."

Connor took in Cody's response and facial expression, trying to read between the lines.

"Can you account for your time in any way?" he asked. "Any messages sent, activities, anyone you spoke to?"

"I was—I was here. Home alone, with Tracy."

"Did you see anyone else that night, speak to anyone else?"

Cody's eyes flickered with uncertainty before answering. "No, I didn't see or speak to anyone else."

"Are you sure about that, Cody? Your alibi is the only thing that's keeping you from being a suspect in a murder investigation."

Cody's eyes widened in shock. "What murder investigation? I don't know anything about that."

"There's been a series of murders. All the victims were recent customers at the diner."

Now Cody looked frantic with stress. "I don't know what to say. I was home alone with Tracy. We made dinner, and we watched a couple of things on television, we made some plans for the party. It was just a normal night, but only Tracy can confirm that."

Connor hesitated.

This was always a tricky situation to negotiate, and it wasn't the first time it had happened. Cody had no alibi and couldn't account for his actions. The presence of a girlfriend was not enough to clear him. He needed a more impartial source for that.

But sometimes, people didn't have alibis and it was as simple as that.

Connor's instincts told him that Cody was telling the truth. He had seen enough liars in his line of work to be able to pick up on the subtleties of deception. However, he couldn't just take Cody's word for it. He needed to talk to Tracy and get at least some confirmation of his alibi.

"Okay. I want to speak to Tracy," he said. He wasn't going to give them any time alone. He wanted to hear her version first. Connor strode downstairs and back into the poker room.

"Tracy?" he asked, and as he'd expected, the woman who'd been sitting next to Cody stood up.

"That's me," she said warily, tugging her velvet jacket into place.

Connor beckoned Cody back into the room, and then led the way upstairs again, this time with Tracy following.

“What were your movements on Wednesday?” he asked.

Tracy looked nervous as she answered. “I was at work all day, I got off at about five, and went straight home to Cody.”

“And you can confirm that he was home with you the entire evening?” Connor asked.

“Yes, we watched TV, cooked dinner, chatted about the party. We were together the whole time,” Tracy said, her voice shaking slightly. “I texted a few people to ask them if they could be there.”

Connor frowned.

He couldn’t bring Cody in just for want of an alibi. He didn’t have recent scars on his face, or on his hands. Connor had checked.

It might be sufficient to tell him to go to the police station tomorrow and give a DNA sample, so they could match it with any analysis taken from Priscilla, who had fought and struggled. He could do that, and warn him not to leave town until the investigation had wrapped up.

To be totally sure, though, Connor decided he should call Cami first.

She might have uncovered something in the course of her investigation that led to a stronger suspect than Cody.

Connor called her number, hoping to touch base with her and be able to make his final decision.

But she didn’t pick up.

To his consternation, since they’d promised to stay in communication and he knew she’d have her phone with her, he listened to it ring and ring.

Coldness clenched at his stomach. Despite his best efforts to keep her safe, something must have gone wrong.

# CHAPTER TWENTY FOUR

Cami clenched her fists in astonishment, staring at the contents of the "Private" folder that she'd been able, finally, to access.

Rows and rows of names and addresses and phone numbers. They were entered neatly, in date order. The list was about three months old, and up to forty or fifty names had been added each day. They all looked to be customers of the diner.

"They must be customers!" she said. "What else could they be?"

There was a way she could check, of course.

Feeling as if her heart was in her throat with excitement at this lead, Cami scrolled down. It didn't take her long to reach the most recent day that Priscilla had been at the diner.

There she was! Her name was there.

And her address. Her home address. And her phone number. Everything. All of Priscilla's information, set out in a private folder, in Tom Gaynor's computer.

Cami breathed hard, her mind racing. She wished Connor was here. He was confronting a suspect and she didn't know if she should call him to tell him about this.

She had to figure out what to do, and how she should deal with this bombshell. No point in calling him until she had more of the facts straight.

Trying to keep calm, she checked off her options on her fingers.

"Okay," she said. "Firstly, how was this information obtained? I need to find that out. This puts the owner in the spotlight again, but he's worked at the diner every day. Can I confirm that?" She paused. "Yes, I can. I can confirm if he was here on Wednesday, because there's a camera pointing at the till. He seems to be back and forth the whole time around that till."

It might be a good idea to do that immediately, Cami thought, her heart pounding harder as she wondered if he'd told a lie to them, a lie that they'd believed. He'd brought her coffee and soda but he could be the killer. She could be shut away in the killer's office right now. That was a precarious situation to be in.

Quickly, Cami accessed the camera footage and ran it back to Wednesday evening.

She watched carefully as the footage fast-forwarded.

Then she let out a long sigh of relief. Gaynor had told them the truth. He'd been at the till, bustling around, taking payments, greeting customers, just about nonstop through the whole of Wednesday, right up until closing time. There'd been a few breaks of ten to twenty minutes when he'd obviously been eating, or checking tables, or in the office, but those had not been long enough for him to have driven to Kate's house and grabbed her. She lived twenty minutes away from this diner.

So, Gaynor was cleared.

But now the question remained—the million-dollar question—how had he gotten hold of all those customer details, and what were they doing in a private folder on his computer?

Cami perched on the edge of her chair, thinking frantically. She needed to preserve the evidence first. She couldn't risk him deleting the folder or destroying it, and then claiming it had never existed.

The first thing she should do was copy it.

Immediately, she did just that, sending the data to the cloud. This case had taught her that people in possession of information that could bury them would rush to delete it at all costs.

Now, it was copied to the cloud. And now, she couldn't hide away in this office any longer. She needed to get out there and ask Gaynor what the hell was going on with this.

Cami opened the door, hoping that this would go well.

Mr. Gaynor was at the till, ringing up a payment, warmly greeting an incoming couple, but she could hear an edge of worry in his tone that hadn't been there before.

Was it just because the police were poking around in his office? Or was there a more serious reason for it? As soon as he'd finished, she called out to him, speaking loud to be heard over the Queen ballad that was playing.

"Mr. Gaynor? I need to find something out."

He turned to her, stress deepening the lines on his otherwise pleasant-looking face. "Sure. What is it?" he asked.

Cami took a deep breath and asked in a calm tone, "I accessed your computer and found a private folder with all the customers' info, including their home addresses and phone numbers and even what they ordered. Can you explain why that information is there?"

Gaynor's face went from worried to alarmed, "I…uh…that's confidential information. It's only meant for the diner's records. I didn't think anyone would access it. I put a password on that folder so that it would remain secure."

Cami raised a skeptical eyebrow. "I got into it and saw it. Why would you need to keep customers' home addresses and phone numbers on file, Mr. Gaynor? And how did you get hold of them?"

He sighed. "It's a competition we have been running."

That was an unexpected answer. "What competition is this?"

He stepped away from the till, talking in a low, confidential tone. "Look, it's been hugely successful. We ask customers to fill in their info, and rate what they ordered, and at the end of every week, we do a lucky draw for a prize." He gestured to the windows. "We have a lot of sponsors and we've had some great prizes. Travel bags, phones, cosmetic kits, kids' toys. It's created a lot of fun and excitement and massive goodwill for the diner and the sponsors, and it gives us feedback on our food, so we've been able to keep it going for months. The prizes get delivered and everyone's been very happy to give their info."

"How exactly do they give the info?" Cami asked.

"We have a competition form that we send to the table with the menus. Most people fill it in and give it back to us with their payment. If they ask, we do reassure them that it's kept confidential. I mean, I don't leave the forms lying around. I put the data in every single day, and once a week, I do a randomized draw from the names using an app. One form per entry, so regular customers get a better chance."

"And you keep all the details on file?" she asked.

"Yes," he replied. "I just thought it made sense to keep all the details in one place. I didn't think it would be a problem. And they did give permission for the diner to contact them. Which of course, also helps with our marketing, I mean, they do check a box to say we can add them to our email mailing list," he explained anxiously.

"Who has access to your computer?" she asked.

"Only me," he said firmly. "My office is locked when I'm not in it, and I password protected that folder so that nobody could take our client information, which of course is very valuable."

Cami nodded. He'd taken precautions. But someone had gotten hold of the information all the same.

A hacker, someone who'd been able to log in and crack the password just like she'd done?

That was a possibility she needed to look into, but as the thought crossed her mind, Connor's voice rang in her ears.

*"Maybe it's not high tech, Cami. Maybe it's low tech."*

She took a deep breath. Finally, she saw the other option, the one she'd been on the point of missing.

"These forms," she said. "What do you do with them when you've input all the information?"

"I throw them away, of course," Gaynor said. "I don't accumulate them. I do one lot in the afternoon, and then another lot later in the evening, just before we close."

"Where do you throw them?" she asked.

"I take them outside, and they go into the dumpster." He gestured toward the back of the restaurant.

A dumpster?

The word struck a chilling chord in Cami.

Now, at last, she thought she knew how the killer was working, and how he'd managed to find the addresses of the single women who'd eaten in the evenings here. He'd raided the dumpster, a gold mine of information, with forms from a competition that had been running for months.

A low-tech solution.

And as she realized this, Cami knew that there was a high-tech way she could find him. It was one that she could put into action right now.

## CHAPTER TWENTY FIVE

"Camera footage!" Cami muttered the words, turning back to the screen as her fingers flew.

Not from tonight. Tonight, this killer wouldn't yet have arrived, because the owner only threw the forms away at closing time. But she could access the footage from last night, and the night before. Then she might see him.

This killer had been rooting through the trash. That, she was now sure of. And he'd found what he needed.

Could she see his face? Would there be a way to identify him?

There was the footage from camera two, which overlooked the restaurant's back alley. She clicked on it and accessed the folder.

"Um, ma'am, is there anything I can do to help?" From behind her, Gaynor's voice was twanging with stress. Cami jumped so violently she nearly hit the office's white-painted ceiling. She'd forgotten completely that he was there.

"I think I've gotten what I need," she said, turning to him. "I'm looking at the footage from the second camera. The footage of your back lot."

"That?" He raised his eyebrows. "I'm surprised that's useful to you, but I guess it's helped us, also. We installed it a couple of years ago, after we had a few staff cars broken into, and a couple of attempted thefts of the premises. Folks are desperate. They'll break in to steal staff clothing, the petty cash box. It's prevented a lot of that, but what can you see?"

She showed him. "Look here. On the edge of the footage. There's you, I guess you're throwing away the slips?"

"Yes, that's me." He peered closer. "I can see myself there, throwing the evening's slips away."

"Now, wait. Let's see if we can see what I expect to find," Cami said.

She fast-forwarded the footage. One hour, two hours. Now it was after midnight and the place was quiet, the diner long since closed.

And there he was. A dark figure, dressed in black, a baseball cap pulled low over his eyes.

He lurked around the dumpster, furtively glancing around before diving in. He rummaged through the trash, tossing aside empty containers and food scraps until he found what he was looking for. Working fast he grabbed a handful of papers and stuffed them into his pocket before making a quick getaway.

"That's him," Cami breathed. "That's our guy. But he knows where the camera is and he's not letting us see him."

Not once did the scrounging man glance at the camera. He kept his head low and his back turned away.

Gaynor looked horrified. "I can't believe this is happening in my diner. How could I have let this happen? I thought I was preventing personal information from being stolen!"

"I'm going to see if he was there the previous night, too," Cami said.

She felt a sense of doom descend as the footage picked him up again. He'd been here every night, she guessed. Rooting through those slips, carefully choosing the ones he thought would work for him. He must have a lengthy list of potential victims by now, and what did they have? Not even a clear sight of him.

She searched another night earlier, nodding grimly as the same figure appeared on the screen. He was there again. This was his ritual. Had he been careless at all? Had he faced the camera even once?

Cami rewound the footage to the moment when the figure first appeared on screen. She watched as he rummaged through the trash. His face was steeped in shadow. He was being careful every step of the way not to be seen.

At that moment, there was a sound of smashing glass from outside the office, and a shriek, followed by raucous cheers from the few remaining customers.

Mr. Gaynor jumped, looking guilty, as if he'd been shirking his duties by watching the footage. "I'd better get back to work," he said, and rushed out of the office.

Now Cami was on her own, watching this killer.

She still had no idea who he was. He could, potentially, be the assistant manager that Connor was now confronting. A staff member could have sneaked back after hours. Or else he could be a customer. All it would take was one lucky visit to the diner for a psychopathic killer to work out that he could use this information. He might have asked one of the waitresses what happened to the forms, wondering if they could be useful to him.

The reality chilled Cami as she thought about the diner's large, bright windows, so well placed to advertise the business.

He could have stared through the windows, seeing that a lot of women felt comfortable eating here, and that if he got their addresses, he could quickly do surveillance and see which ones were single. Those eating dinner at a table for one were a giveaway. He'd just have to find the table number on the form to be sure.

That was what she thought he'd done.

He had gone the lowest of low-tech routes possible. He'd looked through the windows, identifying the tables he needed, the ones where single women were sitting. And then, after dark, at the end of the night, he'd sneaked back to the dumpster for those forms he needed.

She was sure now, that if the forms were no longer available, he'd find another way to get his victims. This was just how he'd started. Now the monster was out, and they had to stop him.

Shivering, she scrolled back another night. And there he was again.

This time, he had been more patient. He'd taken some time. He'd gone through the receipts in a more leisurely way. She could see his fingers touching each one, discarding them. He was actually reading them there.

"Why did he stop doing that?" she asked.

A moment later, thinking back to his timeline, she had her own answer. It was because the police had found the first body.

After that, he'd been much more careful, not wanting to spend time there in case he was caught.

Look at him, going through those slips in that leisurely way, busy deciding on his next victim. He could be stalking one of the women on the slips right now. He could be waiting for her to get home. He could have found his way into her house, just like he'd done with the others.

How could she tell? Was there a way?

Cami let out a shaky sigh. There were too many customers in the diner to warn all of them right now, although she guessed they could all be warned over time. He wasn't fussy in terms of age, and he'd been hunting for probably nearly as long as they'd been doing this prize drawing.

But still, she couldn't stop herself from scrolling back through the footage, looking at his actions, wondering frantically if she could somehow stop him from taking one more. Just one. Who was he looking at here? Who was he planning on stalking?

There he was, paging through the slips with intent. She could see it in his body language. It was as if he was focusing on something he wanted to find. One woman, one in particular. She felt sure of it. As if she was tuning in to his mind.

And then he paused, and he picked the page up. Held it, reading it. And then he shoved it into his pocket, turned, and disappeared from the camera's eye.

She let out a deep, stressed sigh. This had been two nights ago. He'd been planning. He'd been on the hunt. And she was sure that by now, he would have researched his latest victim and be ready to take her.

"There has to be some way I can stop this," Cami said. "Who was that woman? Which form was it? I have all the information here. Surely I can find something?"

She looked again. What was on this slip? She scrolled through, frame by frame. She magnified the footage. It was blurry, but for one split second, the page was in the glow of the restaurant's light.

Cami narrowed her eyes. She had an app that might be able to make more sense of those blurred pixels. She isolated the photo and ran it through her app.

It couldn't tell her much. The camera was too far away, and the lettering much too hazy. The only thing she could see, from this clearer image, was that it was a longer piece of writing on the second line. That was the address line. Cami could see that the address almost filled the field. So it was a long address.

And the name line above? That was very short.

The blurry text, magnified fifty times, didn't allow for any more clarity than that. Out of all the women who'd been there that night, this was as much as she had. Could she tell from the records?

Cami went into the records to see if there was anything that compared to this from that night.

"Long address. Short name." She scrolled down the list, looking for those two variables that were all she had, her only hope of knowing which slip of paper the killer had so unerringly singled out.

There were two possibilities from that night's list.

"It could be this one." Sue Jack, of 91 Middlefields Close, Amber Road. "Or it could be this one." Vera Dann, of 103 Pleasant View Street North.

The other names were all longer. Apart from that, she had nothing more to go on. But Cami decided it would be wisest to call both of them.

With her heart racing, Cami dialed the cell number for Sue Jack.

It rang and rang. She started to feel sick with the tension. And then, a sharp, impatient voice answered.

"Hello. Sue here."

"Sue, my name is Cami Lark. Listen, I need to speak to you urgently. It's—"

"I'm sitting on an airplane and we're about to take off! If it's anything to do with spa bookings, I'll be back after the weekend and you can contact the main office. If it's anything else, can you text me?"

"An airplane?" The gist of the conversation sank in. Sue was okay. She was flying out of Boston. By the time she got back, Cami hoped, they would have caught the killer.

"I'll call you back," she said, feeling relieved.

She hung up and focused on the next name on the list. Vera Dann.

She called that number, feeling even more nervous than when she'd called Sue. Hopefully she'd be in time to warn this woman.

"Hello?" An impatient voice answered.

"Hello, Vera?" Cami felt breathless. She had only a moment to give this warning. "Listen, my name is Cami Lark, and I'm working with the FBI. You may be in danger. Please, are you home?"

"Just getting there. Sorry, I didn't hear what you said. Signal's bad here."

"You're in danger!"

"What was that? I can't hear what you're saying. Listen, can you call back in two minutes and then I'll be inside? This wind's crazy and I'm carrying shopping bags."

"No, wait!"

Cami heard the sound of a key in the lock. Then, a shrill, horrified scream.

And then the line went dead.

# CHAPTER TWENTY SIX

"No!" Cami shouted the word aloud. Her worst fears had been realized. The warning had been too late. Vera Dann had arrived home, and from that scream, she was sure the killer had been waiting.

She needed to get to her! And fast!

Taking a deep breath she tried to quell the panic that was surging inside her. Calm thought would help her now.

First things first. Her address. Where was she?

Trying to stop her hands from shaking, Cami looked up the address. Vera Dann lived eight miles away, in a suburb to the north of the diner.

"Eight miles?" Cami said aloud, her voice shaking. It felt like an insurmountable distance to Vera's house. And the killer wouldn't keep her there. Most likely he would move fast, and right now, he would be taking her somewhere else.

She'd have to move fast, too, and the problem with that was Connor had gone to interview the missing employee, which she now knew was a dead end. Worse still, he'd gone in exactly the opposite direction. He'd headed out to the south of Boston, the outskirts of the city, and would take time to get back.

She couldn't wait for him. She would have to act alone, but she needed a car, and also a means of tracking Vera.

"Her phone?" Cami muttered. "The call was cut off. But maybe the phone's still on?"

She had to hope that the killer had left it on, that he hadn't turned it off in the rush of doing everything else, that she had some time, at least, to follow it, because otherwise Vera would disappear.

"Please, let the phone be on, let it be on."

She had an app that usually worked reliably to track phones, but it sometimes malfunctioned, and would only give a ping back if the phone was moving. Frantically, she entered the phone number into her tracking software and waited, glancing at the screen as she rushed out of the office to the reception area.

"Everything alright?" Gaynor asked, looking in concern at her visibly stressed demeanor.

"No, it's not alright." Cami took a deep breath, trying to come across as coherent despite the intense worry that filled her. "I need to use your car. Will that be possible?"

She waited, breathlessly, for him to reply, but with a thump of her heart, she realized it wasn't going to be so easy.

"I'm afraid it's already in use," he said. "It's on the road. My waiter took it just now to get some supplies from the warehouse. I guess he'll be back in about ten minutes." He looked at her face. "You can't wait ten minutes, I can see that. I can see this is too important."

"Could I use somebody else's?" she asked. "I mean, I have a license, and I think I'm covered by FBI insurance?" She was hazy about how it all worked, but in the sheaf of documents that she'd signed when agreeing to help the FBI in exchange for them dropping the charges, there had been something about being covered while working on a case.

"Yes. Please, go ahead. Ask the other staff, and I'm sure that one of them will help," he said. "If you need me to come and explain the situation, just ask."

A welcoming shout from the entrance door distracted him.

"Evening, Mr. G! You still open?"

He hurried away to greet the couple who'd just arrived. "Yes, yes, we're still open!" he said. "It's late, but you're welcome. Please, sit down."

Cami looked around in a state of high anxiety. She met the eyes of the receptionist, who was staring at her with a worried look.

"Your car?" Cami asked. "Could I borrow your car?"

The woman hesitated, but Cami sensed that she was wavering. She wasn't giving an outright no. She'd clearly sensed Cami's stress, and wanted to help.

"Please. This killer's taken someone else. While I was trying to warn her." Cami blinked furiously, taking a shuddering breath. Now was not the time to allow the emotion she felt at Vera's predicament to overwhelm her.

"Um, well," the receptionist wavered.

"It'll be insured," Cami pleaded. "The FBI covers me on cases. And I'm a licensed driver."

She wasn't an experienced driver. She didn't have a lot of hours behind the wheel, but she'd passed her test and that was what counted, right?

But she could see the receptionist still wasn't convinced.

"If I can get there in time, I can try to save her. This might save her life. You could help save a life!"

It was her last, her final argument. "Together we could do this."

Making up her mind, the receptionist reached into her purse under the counter and slid the keys over to Cami.

"It's the red Honda in the lot out back, near the gate," she said. "Just please bring it back in one piece. My parents gave it to me, and I can't afford a replacement."

"Thank you, thank you, I'll be careful," Cami gabbled, grabbing the keys, getting her laptop bag and her purse, and rushing out before the receptionist could change her mind.

Now, where was Vera headed? Was there a signal on her tracking software?

She checked her phone and saw to her consternation that the program wasn't activating.

"Damn, damn," Cami muttered. Technology wasn't working for her tonight. With the program malfunctioning, she had no idea where Vera was being taken, and no clue about the whereabouts of the kidnapper.

She took a deep breath, trying to keep her panic under control. She could start by driving to Vera's home address, at least. Perhaps, by then, the phone would start to move, or the software would get past its glitch and begin working.

It was only thanks to the combined might of furiously intelligent hackers, intent on taking the use of technology to the edge, that she was capable of tracking the location of an unknown phone, something that was usually the FBI's domain.

And now, she had to call Connor and tell him what was happening. He might have better luck tracking the phone from his side.

Glancing at her phone, Cami realized she'd missed an incoming call from him five minutes ago. In the stress of getting a car, and with her phone on silent, she hadn't seen it. Quickly, she called him back.

"Cami!" His voice was sharp and urgent as he picked up. "What's happening there? You okay? You didn't pick up when I called you. I'm about to leave here. I've just cleared this suspect—for now, anyway."

"Connor, I've found who it is. I've worked out how he's doing this." With a heroic effort, Cami controlled her breathlessness. Panic would only slow things down now. "He's raiding the dumpsters and taking the restaurant's contest forms with client information. I've seen him on camera. And I've found the next person he's targeting."

"You sure?" Connor asked.

"Yes. I worked it out. And I called her to warn her, but I think—I think she got home as I called, and he was waiting. She screamed, and then the call was cut off."

Here was the red Honda. She opened it and climbed inside. It was an older car, but neat and tidy and obviously cared for.

"Okay. Address?"

Cami read it out and heard Connor sigh.

"I'm nearly thirty miles from there. I'll get there as fast as I can, and I'll get the local police there, too. They might be faster than me."

"I'm eight miles away and I've borrowed a car," she said. "I'm going to go there right away, but he'll probably have taken her by then."

"Cami, no!" His voice was sharp. "You can't risk your life chasing after her. You're unarmed and not combat trained."

"Connor, if I can see where her phone's headed, I need to start following it. It'll give us a lead, at any rate. I'm trying to track it but my software is being slow. The point is, he could turn off the phone at any time and then we have no idea where he is."

"No! Wait! Let me get backup to you first," Connor said.

"No! I'm going! Backup can meet me there," Cami shot back. She wanted to obey Connor, but how could she do that when she'd actually heard a victim being taken? The woman's terrified cry still resounded in her mind.

Firmly, she hung up. And then she started the car, driving unsteadily out of the lot, wishing she had more experience behind the wheel. She'd just have to go as fast as she could to the address, and hope that at some stage, her software picked up the phone.

But as she drove, she felt a sense of coldness.

So far he'd held the victims for at least a day. But her phone call might have changed that.

Vera had clearly been on the phone while she opened her front door. The killer might have overheard her, and he might have picked up, from what she said, that someone was trying to warn her.

If he had, then Cami knew with a chill that all bets were off. He wouldn't take her and hold her. He might change his pattern, decide to cut his losses, and kill her immediately, to prevent the police from finding him.

Biting her lip, she mashed her foot on the gas pedal, driving as fast as she dared, hoping that she'd be in time to prevent a disaster.

# CHAPTER TWENTY SEVEN

Cami gripped the wheel as she raced to Vera's house, driving the red Honda as fast as she dared, glancing at her phone every time she got the chance and thought she wouldn't crash if she took her eyes off the road.

Where was the phone? Why wasn't it moving? Why wasn't her tracking software helping her, and what was playing out at Vera's place?

She felt terrified she was too late.

Connor would be setting up his own tracking, and that might work better than her hack, but it would take time. It would probably take ten or fifteen minutes minimum, he'd said.

That was ten or fifteen minutes too long.

She had to get to Vera's place as soon as possible. The thought of Vera being in danger made her sick to her stomach. She couldn't forgive herself if something happened to her because she hadn't warned her in time. She'd said the wrong things. If she'd said the right things, she might have been able to stop her from going inside the house.

She'd failed her and that was the harsh truth.

Now she needed to make up for it.

She turned onto Vera's street, her heart pounding in her chest as she pulled up in front of the house. The front door was closed. The lights were off inside.

And, as she did so, her phone's screen lit up.

"The tracking! It's working!"

At last, she had a location for Vera's phone, and it was on the move.

Cami didn't hesitate.

If that phone was on the move, she needed to follow the signal. She couldn't waste any more time here. She was certain that Vera had been taken. At any rate, she wasn't home. The house was dark. If she'd been home, if she'd been okay, then lights would have been on. And she'd have called Cami back.

The killer had taken her, with her phone and her purse, just like he'd done with the others.

He hadn't turned her phone off yet, and that was a huge stroke of luck for her. But he might do it at any moment. She had to hurry.

Cami sped away from the house, following the signal, glancing between the phone and the road, trying her best not to veer off the road and crash, as she navigated to where it was taking her.

It was late at night, and the signal seemed to be heading on a strange, diagonal trajectory, into town. There weren't many other cars around. Where was he going? She'd assumed that he was holding the women in a more remote setting but now she guessed that a basement room in the middle of town might also be soundproof, and the traffic sounds around during the day might muffle any noises that did leak out.

The signal wasn't moving now. It had stopped at a place ahead, and Cami drove cautiously up to it.

She stared in surprise. This was a building that looked to be in the process of construction. Scaffolding lined the walls. The place was very dark, and when Cami got out, she breathed in the smell of raw concrete.

She couldn't see any cars anywhere. But the signal was definitely stationary here. It was no longer moving.

Climbing out of the car, Cami felt thoroughly spooked. This place was deserted.

She'd disobeyed Connor's instructions to wait, but she knew he'd be racing to meet her, so she needed to tell him where she was now.

Standing close to the car, she texted him her location.

*"Building site. Place looks empty,"* she wrote. *"Waiting for you."*

She didn't expect a reply, because Connor would be speeding to help her. In the meantime, it would be better to lie low.

Except, then the questions began flooding her mind, clamoring for answers.

Why would the killer have left his victims at a building site? As she huddled next to the car door, staring nervously around her, Cami started puzzling over that fact. It didn't make sense. This building site might be deserted now, but it wouldn't be during the day. People would be here, working on it. It would be a hive of activity. The raw concrete smell was strong. It didn't seem like an abandoned site.

And in that case, Cami wondered with a chill, what if it was a trap? Had the killer lured her here?

Or maybe not a trap. Maybe it was a cutoff strategy.

He might not have expected Cami to arrive, but he might have expected the police to be on his trail.

Now her brain was racing ahead. If the killer had heard Vera speaking on the phone, he could have realized she was being warned. Perhaps he'd picked up enough of the conversation to get the gist of that. And that might have been why he and the phone had come here. The aim was to mislead the police and to provide a false trail for them to follow.

If he was doing this, then he might be planning to dump the phone somewhere in this building site and then leave. That way, the police would be searching this site for hours and days, looking for Vera in the ditches and foundations and underneath all that freshly poured concrete, and he'd be free and clear.

She'd gotten here more quickly than the police. Cami didn't think that he would have expected to be so closely followed. Maybe that gave her the edge she needed.

Dump the phone and run, taking his victim to her planned location. Had that been his objective? If he was here and he was doing this, she needed to see where he went next. It might be the only chance she got. If he was still here, and she glimpsed him leaving, she could follow.

Summoning all her courage, knowing that if she was fast, it might make all the difference, Cami tiptoed away from the car and started walking quietly around the building site. Fear bubbled inside her and she did her best to suppress it, trying to cling to logical thought instead.

She didn't have a flashlight, only the light on her phone, but she didn't want to use it because it might draw attention to her and she didn't want that.

The tracking app on her phone was still working. It was telling her the phone was here, somewhere in this site, and that she was getting closer to it with every step.

Now, she was heading inside the building, through a rudimentary entrance that was no more than a concrete archway, and down a passage. Ahead, a bridge of two long steel planks led over a massive gap that seemed to plummet for stories below. For that, she had to use her phone's light. There were no railings, nothing but the planks and the abyss yawning, and as she crossed, one of the planks shifted and her foot slipped.

Her entire stomach lurched and she felt as if it plummeted down the abyss. Her arms windmilled, adrenaline flooded her so sharply that it was sickening. And then she regained her balance and finished crossing, with her heart pounding, shaking all over when her feet touched solid ground again.

"I'm going to guess he came in another way," she whispered to herself, in an effort to pull herself together, but still feeling utterly shocked by that near miss.

Now she was in the depths of the building, with a concrete ceiling shutting out the sky and pillars at intervals. It was light enough to see where she was going—just.

And it was light enough to see something else beyond, in exactly the direction that the phone locator was taking her.

A crumpled form, lying on the ground. She caught the bright flare of a blue jacket, an arm flung over the head.

She'd been wrong. Totally wrong.

This wasn't a cutoff. He'd left her here!

Was she alive?

Cami rushed forward, anxiety flooding her as she wondered whether she'd be reaching an unconscious but alive victim, or kneeling down to discover a cold, lifeless corpse.

The answer was neither.

As she bent, the figure on the ground turned around, shifted its arm, and cold, implacable eyes stared into hers.

Men's eyes. This was no woman! It was a blue business suit that he was wearing, and a lime-green tie. And his face had scars on it, fresh scrapes and scabs on the cheeks. He raised his head and the next moment, impossibly swift, iron hands closed around Cami's throat.

It hadn't been a cutoff. That was her last thought, as her world was swallowed by a pounding darkness.

It had been a trap.

# CHAPTER TWENTY EIGHT

Cami woke to bumping, jolting darkness.

Where was she? What had happened?

Terror flared inside her as she replayed the last thing she remembered. The scarred face of the killer. Steel hands that had clamped around her neck, the blood pounding in her head, her brain starved of oxygen and blackness flooding her.

Now she had a horrible headache, as if from a nasty hangover. Her throat was sore and hoarse, but she was alive and she was thinking clearly.

The problem was that she was trapped in the dark.

Her hands were tied behind her back. Her legs were bound. She was being taken somewhere, in the back of a car, or more likely a van, in total darkness.

Her brain couldn't accept this. She felt the switches being thrown, one after the other, an inexorable cascade. Switches that would result in a state of blind terror.

Okay, Cami told herself. Okay, this is scary. Petrifying, in fact. But you need to think your way out of it, or you're going to die, and you're not going to be able to save anyone else. He'll keep doing this! He'll find another hunting ground and other victims, just like you.

She'd never been in this situation before, never had to battle for her own sanity while being taken on a hell ride.

Logical steps, Cami told herself. Just like what she went through when starting to write a program. Keep it logical. Let one step lead to the next.

Okay. First things first. Why was it so dark?

She wasn't blindfolded. So the darkness must be because the trunk was totally sealed. There might be windows, but if so, they were painted over. And she couldn't check that with her hands tied. That was why she was rattling around, sliding on the carpet as the van swung around the corners.

However, the advantage was that because the back was sealed, whoever was driving couldn't see her. She was invisible to them. This man had dumped her inside, and now he was setting off to wherever he was going. When he got there, he'd take her out, but until then, he couldn't see her.

The ties on her wrists and ankles were tight and painful. Would struggling help, or would it pull the knots tighter? Could she reach the knots with her fingers? She couldn't, and they felt very tight already.

But as she was struggling, her shoulders burning, doing her best to try to fight her way out of these ties, the vehicle turned another corner and this time, Cami really did let out a muffled shriek of horror.

She'd just bumped up against a body.

Not a body. A living person, one who let out the same horrified whimper to feel Cami there.

Connections sparked in her mind.

"Vera?" she whispered. "Is that you?"

"How do you know who I am?" the woman replied, in a shaky, hysterical voice. "What happened? What the hell is going on? That guy—he was in my house, he came to the door when I opened it. It was like he was living there. And then he just attacked me."

She was beside herself with terror and Cami knew that if they were going to get anywhere, she had to talk this woman down.

"Listen," she hissed. "Panicking won't help. Just breathe deeply and let's figure out a way out of this as fast as we can."

"How? My hands are tied behind my back!"

"So are mine." But as she had the thought, Cami realized there might be a way. Her wrists were tied. But her fingers were free. If she could get her hands to Vera's knots, she might be able to unpick them. And if Vera's hands were free, then she could help Cami in turn.

"Stay still," she said. "I'm going to try to undo your knots."

It was easier said than done in the buffeting darkness, but Cami knew she had everything to lose. Gritting her teeth, she braced herself against the side of the van, managing to get some purchase with her trussed legs against the side. She wriggled and writhed, and then, she felt Vera's hands against hers. Her fingers were cold. Cami gave her hand a squeeze. One more wriggle and she'd be higher, able to touch Vera's wrist with her fingers.

"Okay. Here I am. Now let's see if I can get this knot undone," she said. It was pulled viciously tight, but she tugged determinedly at it, working it one way and then the other, doing her best to loosen it. Working blind, with her hands behind her back, was difficult, but not impossible. She wasn't going to let it be.

There. She'd gotten a loop she could get her finger into. But at that moment, the van stopped with a jolt and she was spun away.

Cami swore softly as she collided with the side of the van, and the rope was ripped out of her fragile grasp. If this was the end of the journey then they were finished, they'd lost. There wouldn't be time to get back and try again.

But the van started moving again and she let out a breath of relief.

"Hang on. I'm coming back," she said, writhing and wriggling all over again to get back in position.

There was the rope, and there was the loop. And this time, when she pulled it, she felt the knot unravel.

"I'm doing it," she hissed. "I've got it. Your hands should be free now. Just tug and pull and that rope should unwind."

"It isn't. It's still tight!" Then, in a surprised tone, Vera added, "Oh, okay. Yes, it's coming off. It's off."

"Quickly, do mine," Cami pleaded. Vera was still in a state of panic and until Cami got her own hands untied, she didn't think they were going to get very far. "Find the knot, and just keep on working at it, wriggle it back and forth. You should be able to. I know you can," she encouraged her.

She felt Vera's hands at the knots. Felt her fingers tugging.

"It's so tight, I don't know if I can loosen it," she said, half sobbing.

"Just keep trying," Cami said, wanting to scream with frustration.

And then, suddenly, she felt the blessed relief of the knot pulling loose, and she moved her hands, reaching them around to the front of her body, easing her aching shoulders as the blood flowed back into her fingers.

"Well done," she said. "Now, how do we get out of here?"

It was so dark. Total pitch darkness. She felt her way, her hands exploring the back of the truck, looking for a catch that might open it, or a handle, or something. But there was nothing. They weren't getting out of this cage.

Cami's heart sank as she realized they were trapped. There was no way out of the van, no matter how hard she searched. There were windows at the back, but they were blacked out, and there were no visible openings except the door that was impossible to break. They were like rats in a trap.

Her phone wasn't in her pocket. It wasn't on her at all. Feeling around, she couldn't find it anywhere in the back of the van. Cami felt naked without her phone. Being without it was worse than having her arms tied behind her back. Although, maybe not.

She tugged at the knots around her ankles, loosening them, working them open.

“What are we going to do?” Vera’s voice trembled with fear.

Cami thought about what they could do. What they had. No high tech, no phone, no ability to use tech to help her.

This was something totally unfamiliar to her, having to devise a low-tech solution. But programmer’s logic worked that way. With a program, you took what you had, and you devised a solution. She could apply logic to her current circumstances, with or without tech to help her. She had a problem and had to find a solution, based on what was available to her.

What did she have? She had a van, and a carpeted floor.

Under the carpeted floor? Tools?

With a sudden rush of inspiration, Cami found the edge of the carpet with her hand and tugged at it. It peeled upward, and underneath, she felt the hard rubbery shape of the spare tire. She felt a big, folded tarpaulin and the thick plastic made her shiver, because she could imagine why it was there and what it had been used for.

And something else, as well.

A wrench. A heavy, steel wrench.

As she felt its weight, and the metal points on its edges, Cami’s mind started working.

It was risky, and it might land them in a heap of trouble, but if her plan succeeded, then it would get them both to safety.

Time to put her plan into action. From now, every second was going to count.

# CHAPTER TWENTY NINE

"Okay. So, you get what we need to do?" Cami asked Vera, whispering the words. She'd told her twice. The first time she thought her words had just bounced off the other woman's panic. The second time she hoped they'd sunk in.

"Yes, I get it."

Cami grabbed her arm, squeezing it gently, hoping she could trust her to do what she needed to. This was a completely new dimension for her. She was having difficulty seeing herself in this role. She was tech. She stayed behind the scenes. She programmed and hacked her way to resolutions. It was a lonely game. Trust was easily earned in tech, because the coding proved it right or wrong. She trusted her fellow coders and her fellow hackers.

Trust didn't hinge on unknown variables, the way it was doing now.

This was way out of her area of expertise, but the problem was, right now, there was nothing inside her area of expertise.

She was far beyond her comfort zone. But she needed to survive this. Just long enough to get a phone in her hand.

"We're going to do it, okay? As we planned? And it's going to work fine for us."

"Yes, it will," Vera said, and Cami thought her pep talk had worked, because Vera sounded encouraged.

Cami waited. She needed to listen now, and listen hard. Because she wanted a moment where the car wasn't moving too fast. She had the feeling they were on a deserted stretch of road, because she hadn't heard any other cars for a while. She couldn't rely on any other motorists being around, or noticing, or helping. This was going to be just him and them.

Okay, now would be good. There wasn't a lot of engine noise, and although they were moving, she didn't think it was fast.

She swung her hand back, holding the wrench. And then she flung it forward, toward the black-painted window, as fast and hard as she could, while still keeping hold of it.

The wrench smashed through the glass in a burst of fragments. A hole exploded in the blackness, and muted light rushed in. It seemed almost blinding after the dark.

She'd done it! Part one was over. Now they needed to take this to its conclusion.

She drew the wrench back again. Hammered at the glass again, gouging out a space. Gasping with the effort, Vera reached through. She grabbed the door handle. She twisted it. And it opened. The door swung wide, and Cami grabbed onto Vera's hand, so that she didn't fall out of the van.

"We got it! We got it," Cami gasped. Vera had done her part. And now, if she'd gotten this right, all they had to do was wait.

The van screeched to a stop, slewing and fishtailing. Cami was unseated from her crouched position at the door and went sprawling backward. She hastily scrambled to the door again.

The minute the van stopped, they were on the move.

Bursting through the back doors, out and into the night.

They were on a deserted country road, with only a few twinkling lights in the distance, and a cloud-veiled three-quarter moon overhead. It was the perfect setting for two panicked victims to try to make a run into the darkness. Fleeing into the night—and captured swiftly by the killer. He would have speed and strength on his side, a powerful flashlight, a van, and knowledge of the terrain.

Perhaps even a gun.

All those reasons were why Cami was *not* going to run into the darkness. She was doing exactly the opposite. She was going to do the one thing he wouldn't expect.

As soon as she and Vera had burst out of the van, they crept around it, hugging the righthand side, staying close to it so that it shielded them from sight.

She hoped she'd correctly predicted what would happen next.

The killer wrenched the driver's door open. They heard him swear, loudly and angrily. Footsteps stormed to the back of the car, and then he gasped.

"Stay low," Cami breathed.

The footsteps returned to the driver's door. He reached inside, came out with exactly the sort of powerful flashlight she'd thought he would have.

Its beam lit up the side of the road, shining on tangled grass and bushy trees. This was exactly the terrain that two fleeing women might use to escape. No wonder he was scrutinizing it carefully.

Except they weren't using it. Instead, Cami and Vera were creeping around the car, now passing the hood, getting to the driver's side as quickly and quietly as they could.

And then Vera was in, scrambling to the passenger's side, making space for Cami to get in.

Were the keys in the ignition?

A massive bolt of relief. He'd left them there. That was good, because this wasn't an electric car and she had no idea how to hotwire a normal ignition.

Were the phones there? Yes, they were there. In the cubbyhole.

Now for the next part of the plan. The getaway.

"You ready?" she breathed to Vera.

The woman was slim, with porcelain skin and long, blond hair. Her high-cheekboned face looked haunted in the dim light, but now that she'd recovered from her shock, there was fire in her eyes.

"Hell, yes," she whispered. "Let's go."

Cami slammed the door. Turned the key in the ignition. Started it up. It was important to do all these things as fast as possible, because they were noisy and the minute he heard, he would react.

Central locking. She punched the button. She didn't want him wrenching open the driver's door. The back door of the van was still open but that was okay. You couldn't access the front cab from there.

"Are we going to go now?" Vera asked. "We need to get out of here, hon. You've done great, but now let's get away!"

"Not yet," Cami said. She so badly wanted to speed off, but she kept seeing Connor's face in her mind, and Ethan's face, too. She knew what they would have done. And she needed to do it, too. Or at any rate, she had to try.

"Why not yet?" Vera sounded incredulous.

"One last thing to do here," she said.

And then she pressed the accelerator, hearing his cry of rage and seeing the flashlight veer in their direction.

The plan was almost complete. They could floor it now and be safe. Nobody would ever blame them for escaping. She'd saved the victim, saved a life, but Cami had another solution in mind.

She didn't floor it. Instead, she swerved along the road, veering in a zigzag path at almost a walking speed, letting the car coast onto the grass and then back onto the blacktop and then over the middle line, and then back again. She wanted it to look like the driver was badly injured, or paralyzed by terror, or didn't know how to drive.

She hoped that the signs of a weakened prey would draw the predator in. And now, she had to be ready. What would he try?

She glanced in the wing mirror, saw the flashlight bobbing and bouncing, heard his frantic footsteps. He was giving chase, following the car, ready to wrench open the door and drag them out, desperate to get them, to complete his deadly mission no matter what it took.

Cami knew this would be tough, and it wasn't something she'd done before. But it was the only way.

She watched, her hand tensed on the gear lever, her foot ready.

And when the flashlight was bobbing, big and bright in her side mirror, she floored it, swerving into him as fast and hard as she could.

She gritted her teeth as she waited for the impact.

It was nothing more than a bump, but it was enough.

Her steering hadn't been great, her coordination less so, but it had done the job. The back bumper of the car clipped him, hitting his leg, and he sprawled to the ground, clutching it, groaning.

"It was a trap," she whispered. "And you walked right in."

Then she grabbed her phone, turned it on, and dialed Connor's number.

# CHAPTER THIRTY

"This is his lair?"

With foot covers and head covers in place, Cami stared, horrified, at the underground room in the small deserted farmhouse where they had immediately driven after the killer had been arrested.

His name was Emmett Miller, and his recorded address was in the system. Miller lived in the family home that had been on the record for generations. But he'd never live there again. Cami's well-timed swerve had broken his leg, and now he was in the hospital, under a heavy police guard. DNA samples had already been taken.

She'd been updated on this while driving to his house, in the car with Connor, relieved to be in the passenger seat again. She'd sat in apologetic silence as he'd given her a heartfelt telling off for disobeying his orders. Then he'd thanked her for her bravery and for taking down the killer.

One of the police officers had returned the red Honda—undamaged—to the diner and back to its rightful owner. Connor had promised Cami that he'd send the receptionist flowers and chocolates to thank her for her kindness and trust.

The local police had taken Vera to the police station to interview her, and would then be escorting her to a friend's house for the night, from where she'd go home tomorrow.

Cami felt relieved beyond measure that neither Vera nor she had ended up in this underground prison, on a small farm miles from anywhere, with walls so thick and dense they muffled all sound.

"This is what you put an end to," Connor said. "It was thanks to your guts and your quick thinking that we could get him."

"I didn't use any technology," she said. "Anyone could have done it, and probably better than me."

Connor shook his head. "You thought the situation through, you used what was at hand, you acted with courage, and you made sure the killer was caught. That's tech, in my book," he said approvingly.

The room had peepholes drilled into the wall. Inside was a bed, a basic bathroom with a nonfunctional tap, and a few items of furniture.

And outside it was a stash of clothing and furniture. Top-quality men's clothing from leading designers. And piles of old, shabby clothing.

"He dressed in those new clothes," Cami told Connor. "That's what Vera said he did at her house. He dressed in the smart suits and he met them at their front doors. And then he forced them to wear the shabby men's clothes. As a sort of humiliation. Maybe he was trying to move away from who he'd used to be."

And the items of furniture? Cami was going to take a guess that they had replicated what was in the victims' homes. In a weird way, he'd been recreating their lives.

That was what he'd been doing.

Connor's radio crackled. He was in touch with the FBI office, and they were researching this address, looking for past crimes, getting some background on the family.

"Seems that Emmett Miller had an older sister who died when he was sixteen from causes unknown. They think she overdosed and drowned in the bath, but there was always a question mark over it. His mother spent years in prison," Connor told her. "There were a few visits from child support over the years, but nothing came of it. His mother died last year, I believe, and perhaps that's what triggered a psychotic break."

Cami nodded somberly.

The one thing she did notice about this house was the complete absence of tech. There were no cameras, there was nothing smart in the home whatsoever. Emmett hadn't even owned a computer. His phone was a basic, old-model phone, untrackable through GPS.

Going through the trash had been the lowest of low-tech solutions, and how he'd found his victims. Cami didn't think that tech could have solved this crime. Not with this killer and these circumstances. She'd just been lucky enough to have tracked one of the victims' phones before he turned it off, like he'd turned off the others. And the only reason she'd been able to do that was because he'd tried to set a trap for her.

A trap that had backfired.

Connor shifted his feet and checked the time.

"It's after midnight," he said. "Forensics are wrapping up here, so we'd better get home. Come on. I'll drop you at MIT.

"Thanks."

Cami turned away. She followed Connor upstairs, thinking of the complexity of this case. A killer, born into a dysfunctional family, scarred from his childhood experiences. What chance did he have to be normal in such an environment? She was sure that the mother had kept him prisoner in just the same way that he'd held his own hostages.

But while being scarred was inevitable, Cami knew that becoming a killer had been his own choice. He'd made that decision and picked the deadly path.

As she and Connor drove back in thoughtful silence, Cami wondered again what her mother had been calling about. Looking at that sad basement room, and realizing how bad an abusive family environment could be, was strangely making her feel more thankful for what she'd had. Yes, her dad had been domineering and her mother too silent, she and her sister had been rebels, and she'd turned her back on them after Jenna had disappeared.

But maybe it was time to fix that relationship.

She would try again tomorrow, she decided. She'd try and call her mom again, and this time, maybe, she'd leave a message.

And in the meantime, there were other calls to make.

"I haven't forgotten about Jacenta," she told Connor, as he pulled up outside the gates of MIT. "I'm going to call her first thing tomorrow and set up that coffee date."

He nodded approvingly. "Good," he said. "Let me know how it goes after you've spoken to her. And what she advises."

"I will."

"Thanks again for today," he told her.

Cami climbed out of the car, feeling a mix of trepidation and resolve at the thought of that coffee date, and what it would involve. She'd need to tell her parole officer everything, in confidence, and get her guidance about what to do next.

She hoped it wouldn't backfire on her.

Cami had a nasty feeling, in fact a certainty, that there was more to this situation than she yet realized, and that she was only scratching the surface of something that might go deeper than she feared.

# EPILOGUE

Cami couldn't believe how deeply she'd slept last night. Now, at ten a.m., she felt ready to face the challenges that today would bring. Starting with the coffee date with Jacenta. She'd set that up for the afternoon, but as she walked to the bus stop, there was another destination she had to visit first.

She felt intensely nervous about the meeting ahead, but hopefully it would be a chance to get more information, and a better picture of what was happening.

She was off to see Liam Treverton. He'd replied in the night, messaging back on the command console of his smart home, and the answer was short and simple.

*"We can talk. But u need to be careful, they r watching me. 11 am today, Coffee House down rd frm my place? Inside table."*

"Will do."

Cami reread the message, with paranoia surging inside her again. Liam was scared, and she knew he was scared for a reason.

Coffee house. She'd be there.

But then, as Cami checked it again, the message was erased. As she watched.

The lettering was removed, word by word. And a new message appeared.

*"Change of plan. Come here. To my house. Same time, 11 am. I'll be inside."*

Cami frowned down at the words.

He was changing the plan, to his own house? Was he scared of being seen in public at all? What was happening? Why his place?

She guessed it was for the best, and that he'd figured out this was the most secure venue, but even so, it felt odd to her.

Was it just her? Was she being unreasonable?

Wanting to bounce her feelings off the other person who was interconnected with this case, and get his input, Cami quickly called Kieran.

"Hey, Cami," he answered, picking up almost immediately. "What's happening? Any news?"

She sighed, feeling conflicted again about this message.

"Kieran, it's weird. He did write back on his command console."

"And what did he say?"

"He first said he'd meet me at the coffee house down the road from where he lives. That message came through last night sometime, when I was asleep. I was helping with a case the whole of yesterday."

"Okay." Kieran sounded thoughtful. "So that was the plan. And then? Has something happened since then?"

"Yes," Cami said. "As I was reading the message, it was erased, and he said he wants to meet at his house instead. Same time. Eleven a.m."

"You think there's something off about that?" Kieran asked.

"I don't know," Cami said. "It just feels strange. I mean, why change the plan like that? And why erase the first message? It's like he's trying to hide something."

"Do you know where he lives?" Kieran asked.

"Yes. I've been there."

Inside. To steal a laptop. Better not to bring that up right now.

"Be careful. If you're not comfortable meeting him at his house, then don't."

"I don't feel comfortable, but I'm not sure if it's just me being paranoid," Cami said.

"It could also be him, feeling that it might be more secure in his house," Kieran suggested. "But you need to be cautious, Cami. We're all on edge about this, and there's a reason. There's something bad going on, that's for sure."

"I've got to go," she said. "Whatever's going on, I need to know."

"You want me to come with you? I could meet you there."

Cami thought about that. It was so tempting, but at the same time, she could see it would be a bad idea.

"The problem is it will spook him. He's only expecting me, and he's already changed the venue. Anyone else, and I think he might be too wary to talk."

The bus had arrived. She climbed aboard, still with her phone in her hand, and took her seat at the back.

"Anyway, I'm on my way now," she told him. "I'm on the bus. Just got on."

"Be careful, okay?" Concern was thrumming in his voice. "Call me as soon as you've wrapped things up."

"I will," she said.

The bus navigated its way along the main road, heading out of Boston, away from MIT, and in the direction of the suburb where Liam Treverton's house was located. But Cami realized she was feeling more and more uneasy as she rode. There had been something about those messages that was nagging at her mind, and she felt it was important to pinpoint it.

Was it the language? The first message had been full of abbreviations, the second one had been longer format. But that might just mean he'd had more time in the morning when writing the second message.

Even so, the feeling of unease wouldn't shift, as the bus made its stop-start journey along the main road, cruising along a side road to make a stop at a school and a home for the elderly.

Perhaps she could use what she had—her login to the house—just to check things out, she decided. To put herself at ease. That would be sensible. After all she had access to the control panel and she could see everything in the smart home. Liam hadn't changed his password. And that meant he was okay with her taking a look inside.

Picking up her phone, Cami logged into the home's cameras. There they were. One pointed at the hallway, one outside, one in the living room, and another in the bedroom. There hadn't been so many the last time she was there, especially inside. Liam must have added more cameras—a sign he was feeling in danger, or paranoid.

She couldn't see anything from the camera angles. The house looked empty.

What about the bedroom cam? She clicked on that and took a look.

There was Liam's bedroom. And her eyes widened as she saw him on the bed. His legs, at least. He was lying there. Relaxing. Waiting for her to arrive.

Cami narrowed her eyes.

In running shoes? Wouldn't he take them off if he lay down?

Something was prickling at her instinct now. He was oddly still. She felt, deep inside, that something was wrong.

Logging into the camera's console, she took over the controls and turned the camera, swiveling it so that it pointed at the head of the bed, instead of at the foot, and toward the bedroom door.

And Cami gasped.

As the camera pivoted and the image came into focus, she saw that Liam's head was a bloody mess. The pillow was soaked in crimson. The bedcovers around his head were stained red, a stain that was still spreading and dripping, because this crime had just happened. He'd just been murdered.

Murdered.

Cami's breath came fast in her throat.

Whoever had killed him had known someone was going to arrive. That was why the message had changed. They were waiting there, waiting for her. She would have been killed when she walked inside. Then she'd have been left in the house, like he was.

She was feeling cold all over now, and nausea was clenching her gut. Where were they? Could she see who they were?

If someone was still in there, one of the cameras would pick them up, surely? At least she could find out who they were and take a look at the enemy's face.

She started to turn the other cameras, but at that moment, the display winked out.

Access denied.

The link she'd had was gone. The cameras had been disabled.

Cami sat very still, suppressing sobs, her hands ice cold, as the bus cruised calmly past Liam's stop. For a moment, she saw his house, just like all the others, a pleasant place in tranquil-looking suburbia, undisturbed, with no hint of what was happening inside or who was there, waiting. No cars parked nearby; they'd been too cautious for that. She'd have knocked on the door unsuspectingly.

The bus drove on, with Cami inside, invisible, because nobody expected someone to arrive by bus. Whoever they were, they'd have been looking out for a car.

But now, everything had changed. This was escalating.

Liam was dead. He'd been ready to say more, and now he'd been murdered.

And Cami knew she was no longer safe.

Whoever had killed him would now be hunting for her.

## NOW AVAILABLE!

**JUST HOPE**
**(A Cami Lark FBI Suspense Thriller—Book 8)**

**With her tattoos and piercings, MIT tech genius Cami Lark is rebellious and anti-authoritarian—and finds herself in deep trouble when she hacks the FBI. Faced with the choice of prison or aiding the BAU hunt down serial killers, Cami reluctantly partners. Yet a new case has Cami in over her head: a serial killer is tracking women in a mysterious way, biding his time before taking them and taunting the FBI. Cami wants to outsmart him—but she realizes that she, herself, may just be next.**

"A masterpiece of thriller and mystery."
—Books and Movie Reviews, Roberto Mattos (re Once Gone)

JUST HOPE (A Cami Lark FBI Suspense Thriller—Book 8) is the eighth novel in a new series by #1 bestseller and USA Today bestselling author Blake Pierce, whose bestseller Once Gone (a free download) has received over 7,000 five star ratings and reviews.

A page-turning and harrowing crime thriller featuring a brilliant and tortured FBI agent, the CAMI LARK series is a riveting mystery, packed with non-stop action, suspense, twists and turns, revelations, and driven by a breakneck pace that will keep you flipping pages late into the night. Fans of Rachel Caine, Teresa Driscoll and Robert Dugoni are sure to fall in love.

Future books will be available soon.

"An edge of your seat thriller in a new series that keeps you turning pages! ...So many twists, turns and red herrings… I can't wait to see what happens next."
—Reader review (Her Last Wish)

“A strong, complex story about two FBI agents trying to stop a serial killer. If you want an author to capture your attention and have you guessing, yet trying to put the pieces together, Pierce is your author!”
—Reader review (Her Last Wish)

“A typical Blake Pierce twisting, turning, roller coaster ride suspense thriller. Will have you turning the pages to the last sentence of the last chapter!!!”
—Reader review (City of Prey)

“Right from the start we have an unusual protagonist that I haven't seen done in this genre before. The action is nonstop… A very atmospheric novel that will keep you turning pages well into the wee hours.”
—Reader review (City of Prey)

“Everything that I look for in a book… a great plot, interesting characters, and grabs your interest right away. The book moves along at a breakneck pace and stays that way until the end. Now on go I to book two!”
—Reader review (Girl, Alone)

“Exciting, heart pounding, edge of your seat book… a must read for mystery and suspense readers!”
—Reader review (Girl, Alone)

## Blake Pierce

Blake Pierce is the USA Today bestselling author of the RILEY PAGE mystery series, which includes seventeen books. Blake Pierce is also the author of the MACKENZIE WHITE mystery series, comprising fourteen books; of the AVERY BLACK mystery series, comprising six books; of the KERI LOCKE mystery series, comprising five books; of the MAKING OF RILEY PAIGE mystery series, comprising six books; of the KATE WISE mystery series, comprising seven books; of the CHLOE FINE psychological suspense mystery, comprising six books; of the JESSIE HUNT psychological suspense thriller series, comprising twenty-eight books; of the AU PAIR psychological suspense thriller series, comprising three books; of the ZOE PRIME mystery series, comprising six books; of the ADELE SHARP mystery series, comprising sixteen books, of the EUROPEAN VOYAGE cozy mystery series, comprising six books; of the LAURA FROST FBI suspense thriller, comprising eleven books; of the ELLA DARK FBI suspense thriller, comprising sixteen books (and counting); of the A YEAR IN EUROPE cozy mystery series, comprising nine books, of the AVA GOLD mystery series, comprising six books; of the RACHEL GIFT mystery series, comprising ten books (and counting); of the VALERIE LAW mystery series, comprising nine books (and counting); of the PAIGE KING mystery series, comprising eight books (and counting); of the MAY MOORE mystery series, comprising eleven books; of the CORA SHIELDS mystery series, comprising eight books (and counting); of the NICKY LYONS mystery series, comprising eight books (and counting), of the CAMI LARK mystery series, comprising eight books (and counting), of the AMBER YOUNG mystery series, comprising five books (and counting), of the DAISY FORTUNE mystery series, comprising five books (and counting), of the FIONA RED mystery series, comprising eight books (and counting), of the FAITH BOLD mystery series, comprising eight books (and counting), of the JULIETTE HART mystery series, comprising five books (and counting), of the MORGAN CROSS mystery series, comprising five books (and counting), and of the new FINN WRIGHT mystery series, comprising five books (and counting).

An avid reader and lifelong fan of the mystery and thriller genres, Blake loves to hear from you, so please feel free to visit www.blakepierceauthor.com to learn more and stay in touch.

**BOOKS BY BLAKE PIERCE**

**FINN WRIGHT MYSTERY SERIES**
WHEN YOU'RE MINE (Book #1)
WHEN YOU'RE SAFE (Book #2)
WHEN YOU'RE CLOSE (Book #3)
WHEN YOU'RE SLEEPING (Book #4)
WHEN YOU'RE SANE (Book #5)

**MORGAN CROSS MYSTERY SERIES**
FOR YOU (Book #1)
FOR RAGE (Book #2)
FOR LUST (Book #3)
FOR WRATH (Book #4)
FOREVER (Book #5)

**JULIETTE HART MYSTERY SERIES**
NOTHING TO FEAR (Book #1)
NOTHING THERE (Book #2)
NOTHING WATCHING (Book #3)
NOTHING HIDING (Book #4)
NOTHING LEFT (Book #5)

**FAITH BOLD MYSTERY SERIES**
SO LONG (Book #1)
SO COLD (Book #2)
SO SCARED (Book #3)
SO NORMAL (Book #4)
SO FAR GONE (Book #5)
SO LOST (Book #6)
SO ALONE (Book #7)
SO FORGOTTEN (Book #8)

**FIONA RED MYSTERY SERIES**
LET HER GO (Book #1)
LET HER BE (Book #2)

LET HER HOPE (Book #3)
LET HER WISH (Book #4)
LET HER LIVE (Book #5)
LET HER RUN (Book #6)
LET HER HIDE (Book #7)
LET HER BELIEVE (Book #8)

**DAISY FORTUNE MYSTERY SERIES**
NEED YOU (Book #1)
CLAIM YOU (Book #2)
CRAVE YOU (Book #3)
CHOOSE YOU (Book #4)
CHASE YOU (Book #5)

**AMBER YOUNG MYSTERY SERIES**
ABSENT PITY (Book #1)
ABSENT REMORSE (Book #2)
ABSENT FEELING (Book #3)
ABSENT MERCY (Book #4)
ABSENT REASON (Book #5)

**CAMI LARK MYSTERY SERIES**
JUST ME (Book #1)
JUST OUTSIDE (Book #2)
JUST RIGHT (Book #3)
JUST FORGET (Book #4)
JUST ONCE (Book #5)
JUST HIDE (Book #6)
JUST NOW (Book #7)
JUST HOPE (Book #8)

**NICKY LYONS MYSTERY SERIES**
ALL MINE (Book #1)
ALL HIS (Book #2)
ALL HE SEES (Book #3)
ALL ALONE (Book #4)
ALL FOR ONE (Book #5)
ALL HE TAKES (Book #6)
ALL FOR ME (Book #7)
ALL IN (Book #8)

**CORA SHIELDS MYSTERY SERIES**

UNDONE (Book #1)
UNWANTED (Book #2)
UNHINGED (Book #3)
UNSAID (Book #4)
UNGLUED (Book #5)
UNSTABLE (Book #6)
UNKNOWN (Book #7)
UNAWARE (Book #8)

**MAY MOORE SUSPENSE THRILLER**

NEVER RUN (Book #1)
NEVER TELL (Book #2)
NEVER LIVE (Book #3)
NEVER HIDE (Book #4)
NEVER FORGIVE (Book #5)
NEVER AGAIN (Book #6)
NEVER LOOK BACK (Book #7)
NEVER FORGET (Book #8)
NEVER LET GO (Book #9)
NEVER PRETEND (Book #10)
NEVER HESITATE (Book #11)

**PAIGE KING MYSTERY SERIES**

THE GIRL HE PINED (Book #1)
THE GIRL HE CHOSE (Book #2)
THE GIRL HE TOOK (Book #3)
THE GIRL HE WISHED (Book #4)
THE GIRL HE CROWNED (Book #5)
THE GIRL HE WATCHED (Book #6)
THE GIRL HE WANTED (Book #7)
THE GIRL HE CLAIMED (Book #8)

**VALERIE LAW MYSTERY SERIES**

NO MERCY (Book #1)
NO PITY (Book #2)
NO FEAR (Book #3)
NO SLEEP (Book #4)
NO QUARTER (Book #5)

NO CHANCE (Book #6)
NO REFUGE (Book #7)
NO GRACE (Book #8)
NO ESCAPE (Book #9)

**RACHEL GIFT MYSTERY SERIES**
HER LAST WISH (Book #1)
HER LAST CHANCE (Book #2)
HER LAST HOPE (Book #3)
HER LAST FEAR (Book #4)
HER LAST CHOICE (Book #5)
HER LAST BREATH (Book #6)
HER LAST MISTAKE (Book #7)
HER LAST DESIRE (Book #8)
HER LAST REGRET (Book #9)
HER LAST HOUR (Book #10)

**AVA GOLD MYSTERY SERIES**
CITY OF PREY (Book #1)
CITY OF FEAR (Book #2)
CITY OF BONES (Book #3)
CITY OF GHOSTS (Book #4)
CITY OF DEATH (Book #5)
CITY OF VICE (Book #6)

**A YEAR IN EUROPE**
A MURDER IN PARIS (Book #1)
DEATH IN FLORENCE (Book #2)
VENGEANCE IN VIENNA (Book #3)
A FATALITY IN SPAIN (Book #4)

**ELLA DARK FBI SUSPENSE THRILLER**
GIRL, ALONE (Book #1)
GIRL, TAKEN (Book #2)
GIRL, HUNTED (Book #3)
GIRL, SILENCED (Book #4)
GIRL, VANISHED (Book 5)
GIRL ERASED (Book #6)
GIRL, FORSAKEN (Book #7)
GIRL, TRAPPED (Book #8)

GIRL, EXPENDABLE (Book #9)
GIRL, ESCAPED (Book #10)
GIRL, HIS (Book #11)
GIRL, LURED (Book #12)
GIRL, MISSING (Book #13)
GIRL, UNKNOWN (Book #14)
GIRL, DECEIVED (Book #15)
GIRL, FORLORN (Book #16)

**LAURA FROST FBI SUSPENSE THRILLER**
ALREADY GONE (Book #1)
ALREADY SEEN (Book #2)
ALREADY TRAPPED (Book #3)
ALREADY MISSING (Book #4)
ALREADY DEAD (Book #5)
ALREADY TAKEN (Book #6)
ALREADY CHOSEN (Book #7)
ALREADY LOST (Book #8)
ALREADY HIS (Book #9)
ALREADY LURED (Book #10)
ALREADY COLD (Book #11)

**EUROPEAN VOYAGE COZY MYSTERY SERIES**
MURDER (AND BAKLAVA) (Book #1)
DEATH (AND APPLE STRUDEL) (Book #2)
CRIME (AND LAGER) (Book #3)
MISFORTUNE (AND GOUDA) (Book #4)
CALAMITY (AND A DANISH) (Book #5)
MAYHEM (AND HERRING) (Book #6)

**ADELE SHARP MYSTERY SERIES**
LEFT TO DIE (Book #1)
LEFT TO RUN (Book #2)
LEFT TO HIDE (Book #3)
LEFT TO KILL (Book #4)
LEFT TO MURDER (Book #5)
LEFT TO ENVY (Book #6)
LEFT TO LAPSE (Book #7)
LEFT TO VANISH (Book #8)
LEFT TO HUNT (Book #9)

LEFT TO FEAR (Book #10)
LEFT TO PREY (Book #11)
LEFT TO LURE (Book #12)
LEFT TO CRAVE (Book #13)
LEFT TO LOATHE (Book #14)
LEFT TO HARM (Book #15)
LEFT TO RUIN (Book #16)

**THE AU PAIR SERIES**
ALMOST GONE (Book#1)
ALMOST LOST (Book #2)
ALMOST DEAD (Book #3)

**ZOE PRIME MYSTERY SERIES**
FACE OF DEATH (Book#1)
FACE OF MURDER (Book #2)
FACE OF FEAR (Book #3)
FACE OF MADNESS (Book #4)
FACE OF FURY (Book #5)
FACE OF DARKNESS (Book #6)

**A JESSIE HUNT PSYCHOLOGICAL SUSPENSE SERIES**
THE PERFECT WIFE (Book #1)
THE PERFECT BLOCK (Book #2)
THE PERFECT HOUSE (Book #3)
THE PERFECT SMILE (Book #4)
THE PERFECT LIE (Book #5)
THE PERFECT LOOK (Book #6)
THE PERFECT AFFAIR (Book #7)
THE PERFECT ALIBI (Book #8)
THE PERFECT NEIGHBOR (Book #9)
THE PERFECT DISGUISE (Book #10)
THE PERFECT SECRET (Book #11)
THE PERFECT FAÇADE (Book #12)
THE PERFECT IMPRESSION (Book #13)
THE PERFECT DECEIT (Book #14)
THE PERFECT MISTRESS (Book #15)
THE PERFECT IMAGE (Book #16)
THE PERFECT VEIL (Book #17)
THE PERFECT INDISCRETION (Book #18)

THE PERFECT RUMOR (Book #19)
THE PERFECT COUPLE (Book #20)
THE PERFECT MURDER (Book #21)
THE PERFECT HUSBAND (Book #22)
THE PERFECT SCANDAL (Book #23)
THE PERFECT MASK (Book #24)
THE PERFECT RUSE (Book #25)
THE PERFECT VENEER (Book #26)
THE PERFECT PEOPLE (Book #27)
THE PERFECT WITNESS (Book #28)

**CHLOE FINE PSYCHOLOGICAL SUSPENSE SERIES**
NEXT DOOR (Book #1)
A NEIGHBOR'S LIE (Book #2)
CUL DE SAC (Book #3)
SILENT NEIGHBOR (Book #4)
HOMECOMING (Book #5)
TINTED WINDOWS (Book #6)

**KATE WISE MYSTERY SERIES**
IF SHE KNEW (Book #1)
IF SHE SAW (Book #2)
IF SHE RAN (Book #3)
IF SHE HID (Book #4)
IF SHE FLED (Book #5)
IF SHE FEARED (Book #6)
IF SHE HEARD (Book #7)

**THE MAKING OF RILEY PAIGE SERIES**
WATCHING (Book #1)
WAITING (Book #2)
LURING (Book #3)
TAKING (Book #4)
STALKING (Book #5)
KILLING (Book #6)

**RILEY PAIGE MYSTERY SERIES**
ONCE GONE (Book #1)
ONCE TAKEN (Book #2)
ONCE CRAVED (Book #3)

ONCE LURED (Book #4)
ONCE HUNTED (Book #5)
ONCE PINED (Book #6)
ONCE FORSAKEN (Book #7)
ONCE COLD (Book #8)
ONCE STALKED (Book #9)
ONCE LOST (Book #10)
ONCE BURIED (Book #11)
ONCE BOUND (Book #12)
ONCE TRAPPED (Book #13)
ONCE DORMANT (Book #14)
ONCE SHUNNED (Book #15)
ONCE MISSED (Book #16)
ONCE CHOSEN (Book #17)

**MACKENZIE WHITE MYSTERY SERIES**
BEFORE HE KILLS (Book #1)
BEFORE HE SEES (Book #2)
BEFORE HE COVETS (Book #3)
BEFORE HE TAKES (Book #4)
BEFORE HE NEEDS (Book #5)
BEFORE HE FEELS (Book #6)
BEFORE HE SINS (Book #7)
BEFORE HE HUNTS (Book #8)
BEFORE HE PREYS (Book #9)
BEFORE HE LONGS (Book #10)
BEFORE HE LAPSES (Book #11)
BEFORE HE ENVIES (Book #12)
BEFORE HE STALKS (Book #13)
BEFORE HE HARMS (Book #14)

**AVERY BLACK MYSTERY SERIES**
CAUSE TO KILL (Book #1)
CAUSE TO RUN (Book #2)
CAUSE TO HIDE (Book #3)
CAUSE TO FEAR (Book #4)
CAUSE TO SAVE (Book #5)
CAUSE TO DREAD (Book #6)

**KERI LOCKE MYSTERY SERIES**

A TRACE OF DEATH (Book #1)
A TRACE OF MURDER (Book #2)
A TRACE OF VICE (Book #3)
A TRACE OF CRIME (Book #4)
A TRACE OF HOPE (Book #5)

Made in the USA
Middletown, DE
11 January 2024